Summer Of Angels

A Mystic Bay Mystery
Jody Sharpe

Contents

Angels

Outside the open window the morning air is all washed with angels
American Poet Richard Wilbur (1921-2017)

For my husband Dave

Chapter 1
The Dream

T he old man moves with a walker, slowly to an edge of a swimming pool. Someone is behind him. A hand is on his arm.

He appears to teeter. Will he be pushed in? The old man says, "Angel!"

I wake up with a start, realizing the angel I often see in my dreams has been here again. Usually, the dreams are comforting to me, but not this time. This time she has sent me a vision that is disturbingly crystal clear, sending my heart racing. An old man walks to a pool's edge. Someone is behind him. He starts to teeter. Will he be pushed in by someone? I thought I heard this man say "Angel!" But did I?

I look at the clock, noting it's 4 am. My alarm went off fifteen minutes ago. I'll be late for work if I don't get out of bed. As I take the fastest shower ever, I worry about the dream. The old man, whoever he is, might be pushed into a pool and might drown. Who is he? Knowing this man is out there and the angel showed me this vision is scaring me. Is this a real scenario? My heart quickens as I hurriedly get dressed. I am slightly psychic, but I have never had such a frightening vision in a dream, or in daylight, for that matter. The only psychic vibe I have usually is knowing how TV shows or movies will end, who likes me or not, where my earrings that I can't find are, and those sorts of clairvoyant things. As a meteorologist at my dream job at KHBW, sometimes I can see a weather change before it occurs, but I would never let the public or, of course, my boss know this. They'd think I'm nuts. I can't predict the whole weather forecast anyway. I just get a vibe about it. My name is Gayle Force and I'm a meteorologist for *Good Morning San Francisco*.

Six months ago, I landed my amazing job and moved to Mystic Bay, into the house that had been my parents'. They live in San Diego now and had rented it out for years. I bought the bungalow from my mom and dad for quite a deal. Mystic Bay, a pretty seaside town with an angel and psychic vibe, is about thirty miles south of San Francisco. I've longed to live here for years, since I was born here and lived in this very house for three years before we moved to San Diego. I spent summers here as a child, living with my Aunt Nancy and Uncle Dick, who luckily are my next-door neighbors now.

Finished dressing, I sweep my hair in the usual ponytail I'm known for on TV. I'm dressed in the orange dress and heels I laid out last night and put heavy make-up on with as much finesse as possible. I need to have it caked on for TV.

I feed Maurice, my wise and wonderful, yellow-eyed black cat, take the cup of coffee I've poured, and out the door I go. I drive the twenty-seven miles to the station. Since moving to Mystic Bay, finally, after years of yearning for it, the connection to my aunt and uncle helped. When I interviewed at the station, I knew I would get the job not only with my former employer's recommendation but also with a good word from Breezy Bob Bruce, the head meteorologist and friend of Uncle Dick. I hated to leave my mom and dad and life in San Diego, and my great job at the TV station I worked at for nine years. The station manager offered me more money to stay, but my contract was up and KHBW recruited me for a bigger job.

It was a sign from heaven that Mystic Bay is where I belong. I've known it deep in my heart. It's a town some now call, "Town of Angels," as angels appeared to three children here a few years back.

My best friend, Maggie Greenstreet, who lives there still, was with one of the children who saw an angel. She was a special education teacher and the child spoke her first word after seeing the angel. Her first word was "angel." How beautiful is that? The feel of the town is like no other. Psychics and ordinary folk live together by the sea in this picturesque California town. Lucky for me, Maggie lives not too far from me with her husband, Noah, and new baby, Marshall. We try to have tea or coffee weekly in the afternoons after I get home. I'm wary to tell Maggie about my dream of the old man. But she's a gifted psychic and has seen angels herself. I'll have to tell her at some point.

My mother named me Gayle because she loved the name, as it reminded her of the sea winds of Mystic Bay. When she met Ted when I was one, he adopted me. My father, Joe, died before I was born. I feel his spirit near sometimes and felt, as I grew older, that he approved of Ted adopting me, that it was written in the stars that I would change my last name to wonderful Ted's last name, Force. He's been such a great dad to me. Gayle Force. It's a perfect name for a TV meteorologist, isn't it?

Lost in thought as I drive, thinking about my dream, I wonder who the old man is. Was it just some kind of weird anxiety dream? I push these thoughts out of my mind as I arrive at the station for the five am show. Luckily, every one of my co-workers is friendly. They greet me with, "Good Morning G Force," as my boss, Wes Wentworth, loves goading me about my name.

My weather segment starts: "Good morning, everyone. Well, we are off to a wonderful, misty start on this June first in the Bay Area. Our low clouds today will disappear in a few hours, then ahead only sunshine, light winds at five miles an hour, and clear skies. Highs today all across the region in the low sixties. The moon will be extraordinary tonight as it's a Strawberry Moon. But early tomorrow, a front is moving in with the possibility of rain drops tomorrow and Sunday. Make sure you have tomorrow's raincoats and umbrellas handy, just in hopes. A slight warm-up is coming again next week for sure. So, folks grab your cup of coffee or tea and get ready for a high of 65 today. Wear that sunscreen and hat at the beach as always. Back to you, Mark!"

"Thanks, Gayle," says Mark, the anchor of the show. "Tell us where you'll be reporting from tonight!"

"Mark, I'm excited because tonight, I'll be coming to you live at six and ten with an update on San Francisco's Gala for Somerset House, the housing development for the homeless that has been a role model now for cities across the country. Our own handsome Breezy Bob Bruce will be the MC tonight at the elegant San Francisco Plaza Hotel. It's the highlight of the June Gala season and oh so important for our homeless population. I hope to speak to some of the patrons and professionals who have made the philanthropic accomplishments of Somerset's founder, Dr. Jeremiah Parker, a household name."

"Great, Gayle. Enjoy, and we'll have a segment from you about the Gala tomorrow morning."

What I don't say on TV is that Tory Rios, my best college friend from our San Jose State days, is assistant to Somerset House's new CEO, Evelyn Parker. Evelyn Parker is the younger wife of Dr Jeremiah Parker and running the charity now. I've never met the woman but apparently Doc, as everyone calls Dr. Jeremiah, is recently ailing and Evelyn has taken over. She's the big kahuna now, replacing Doc. According to Tory, Doc's son, Tyler Parker, quit in disgust when Evelyn took over. Everyone thinks he might sue Evelyn, but no one knows what's happening. Tory says Doc's a great man and it's been horrible having him gone from the workplace. I'm glad I'm not in that work mess and I feel bad for Tory. I have listened to her vent about Evelyn since I got my new job. I have advised her to look for another job, but she loves the other people she works with, besides Evelyn, and she is determined to work hard helping the homeless. She's not alone. Most people at work, Tory says, love working with the population, seeing their lives improve. Yet, the only sad part is they fear Evelyn Parker. Behind her back, most workers call her Evil Ev.

———

It's 6 pm and the cocktail and hors d'oeuvres part of the Gala is in full swing as I stand in the lobby interviewing some of the patrons. My cameraman, Saul, is funny as he gestures me to walk over to Evelyn Parker, who obviously is avoiding me. I shake my head and roll my eyes. There is a reason Saul is laughing and why she's avoiding me. I'm sure she'd be ready for any camera, but as funny as Saul and I know it is, I am wearing a sleek, long black dress with rhinestone straps that looks like a way less expensive copy of the exact designer dress she is wearing. We look like twins with the same frock and well, same sort of hair color. Yet, Evelyn's hair is Marilyn Monroe platinum and mine is darker streaks of blonde. I am twenty-five years her junior too, and that makes me giggle. Her hair is neatly swirled in a fabulous chignon. My hair is in the usual ponytail with a rhinestone band around it. Her long dangly diamond earrings, most likely from Tiffany's, catch the dark gleam of a snake-like look in her eyes. My faux diamond hoops are my favorite earrings. Her dress is a little too tight, as is her face lift. I don't mean to be mean, but let me tell you, this woman is a nightmare on any Elm Street for Tory to work for. She always puts Tory down in front of co-workers. "You shouldn't wear that skirt, Tory," she said to her more than once. "It makes your calves look even bigger." Evelyn's behavior is what I refer to as "jealousy in its darkest green." Anyway, I digress; back to my interviewing. I talk with some members of the Board of Directors and the Governor too.

When seated for dinner, I find I'm next to Tory, who looks lovely in a pink satin sheath. She has her wavy black long hair in a ponytail like mine. She worked all day on this fundraising event, called "Butterflies Are Free." Pink and green butterflies are everywhere, with pink roses on each table, and one stem for each female guest is gracefully placed on the mint green napkins. On the other side of me is Dr. Roberto Duff, touted to be best plastic surgeon in San Francisco. He did Evelyn's lift, no doubt. His pretty, much younger wife is a natural beauty, and nice. She gives me a pleasant hello as I introduce myself. She says, "I love watching you in the morning, Gayle. You sparkle like sunshine, everyone says. Welcome to San Francisco!"

"Thank you, so much," I say and then her plastic surgeon husband with the biggest teeth I've ever seen pipes in.

"Oh, yes, you're the fun weather girl on the morning news? You do a great job!" He is smiling big with his shiny grin and his face a little too tight and close to mine. I smile back and say, "Yes, I so love being a meteorologist here in this beautiful town."

As I take a quick sip of the mediocre Chardonnay while our wedge salads are served, tuxedoed Breezy Bob enters the room. Silver-haired Bob looks dapperly handsome as he introduces Evelyn Parker to the loud clapping of the polite one thousand or so attending. I look at Evelyn, noting my slightly psychic radar is high. The woman is on stage now, the new CEO, touting the accomplishments of Somerset House and her "poor, ailing, husband," Doctor Jeremiah Parker. I look up at the slides of him on the giant screen when he was a younger man, when he started this urban project twenty years ago. Then his later photos are shown, and I almost faint in my chair. He's the man in my dream, an old man now, the one being pushed in the pool! Oh my God! My dream angel wants me to save Dr. Jeremiah? Will someone push him in a pool? Is it his pool? Is it his gold-digger of a wife, Evelyn Parker? The thought comes to me loud and clear. That's IT! She plans to harm her ailing hubby!!

Chapter 2
Surprise Visitor

It's midnight and I can't sleep. I hardly could drive home; I was so upset seeing Doc's face on the screen and knowing I'm going to have to act. But when and how? I couldn't eat a thing and I was starving, even leaving my dessert, my favorite flourless chocolate cake. What am I to do now? How will I help Doc? This is a total nightmare. I've never used my intuition in this way. Walking out to the patio, in pj's and a robe, the chilly night is filled with stars and the wind is low. Maurice is in my arms as I look up, saying goodnight to the beautiful strawberry moon, stars, and God. The moon is indeed full as I close my eyes in prayer to help the doctor. I'm startled by whimpering coming from the front of my house. It sounds like a dog and must be Prince, the dog Aunt Nancy and Uncle Dick recently rescued. I run to the door, putting Maurice down, looking out the side window. But the porch light reveals it's not medium-sized Prince at all. It's a little, white, furry dog. I open the door and the dog walks in. I can tell she's a female, and she acts like she owns the place. I bend down and pet the little one, whose fuzzy fur is a tad bit matted. "Poor girl," I say in my best baby dog talk. "You don't have a collar so you must be a stray." Maurice loves dogs and misses my late pug, Lilee, so much that he still sleeps in her bed next to my bed each night. Our dog guest follows me into the kitchen, and I give her some water and a scoop of Lilee's dog food. She seems so thirsty and not so hungry. I knew I'd be getting another dog at some point and have been waiting for a sign, I guess. This is the sign, hopefully. Maybe she's a runaway. How did she get to my house? It's as if someone left her on my doorstep just for me.

After she drinks a lot of water and eats some, I take her outside to go potty. Tomorrow, I'll call Josh, my vet, and take her in. Wondering if she has a chip and belongs to someone, I hope not, for Maurice and I fell in love the moment we saw her little face and cute demeanor. I wash her off the way I wash Maurice, who likes warm wet towel washes. The little dog is still a puppy and seems to love towel washes too. She even lets me check her paws. She trusts me. I dry her off, singing to her like I do Maurice. I can tell the cat and dog have bonded as I turn out the light and get into bed. Little Magic, I name her, for God's strawberry moon brought a little magic into my life tonight. Magic gets into Lilee's old bed like she figured out our bungalow was a Motel Six for dogs. Maurice cuddles next to her as I use the clapper to turn out the light. Thankfully, I feel sleep coming. I'm exhausted and hoping and praying the little dog has found her forever home with us. I thank the angels for the blessings of Magic and Maurice. I say prayers for Doc Parker, for my family, and always for my late father, Joe, who I know watches over me as he sits next to the angels. "Please angels and Dad Joe, if Dr. Jeremiah Parker is really in trouble, help me find an answer. What can I do? Amen."

Chapter 3
Call Of The Wild

When I awake, I realize I didn't dream of Doc Jeremiah or remember dreaming of anything. I pull the covers up and turn toward the little animals sleeping peacefully. Maurice has one paw resting on Magic. How cute -- he is parenting her. When I get up to make the coffee, in comes Maurice followed by his new best friend. We go outside through the patio door on a misty, cold Saturday morning. I think Magic will be easy to housebreak, or she already could be trained. It's 6 am as the sun rises. The birds are chirping in my little yard. I feed the animals and my psychic vibe tells me Magic has found her home. I leave a message at the animal hospital, so the staff knows I'm bringing her in at eight. I'll wait however long I have to because we need to see Dr. Josh today.

But my mind races, turning to the dream of Doc Parker. What to do now? I thought about Doc when I made coffee and of course, always prepared me, I have a plan. I will text Beau Bolton, my college friend and oddly enough, not so long ago, my three-week love interest. Beau is a detective with the San Francisco Police Department. It won't be easy to do, but I'm going to ask his advice. Someone in the police department has to look into this.

It's a pathetic love story, but here goes. Beau and I were just friends in college. In fact, I was dating his fraternal twin brother, Bart, for a year. Going on double dates and to Frat parties, Beau and I became good friends. But on graduation day, Bart startled me by asking me to marry him. He tried to give me his late grandmother's diamond ring. Well, it was at that awkward moment that I realized my psychic mother was right. She knew I had a huge crush on his brother, Beau, all along, and finally admitted it to myself. Bart was upset when I told him I couldn't marry him. "I'm way too young and immature," I said. This was a true statement. Embarrassed, I blurted out, "I need an exciting career first, before thinking of marriage. But you are such a great guy. I am so sorry." He was hurt but we amicably went our separate ways, me back home to San Diego and the brothers back to their home in Hillsboro, the next town over from Mystic Bay. I hadn't heard from either of them for the years I worked in San Diego, but I had a great job as a substitute anchor and weekend meteorologist at a TV station. I dated a lot but no one special. More frogs than princes. Those on-line dating sites didn't work for me. But I had a great life with Maurice and Lilee by my side and I lived close to Mom and Dad. However, I never seemed to get over that unrequited crush on the ever-so-gallantly handsome, Beau Bolton.

Then, a few months ago, I was offered the unexpected opportunity at KHBW in San Francisco. In anticipation of me seeing Beau again, Tory always kept in touch, and she would give me the news of the Bolton brothers. Beau was a big cheese detective with the San Francisco Police, and Bart, a stockbroker, had married a girl we knew casually in college named Amber. When I moved to Mystic Bay, Tory planned a party for me to meet her friends and invited the Bolton brothers. I wasn't worried about Bart but a little scared to see Beau again. Yes, unfortunately, pitter patter went the heart, the crush was still there. He looked amazing and his fun sense of humor was alive and kicking. He arrived at the party late in a tight T-shirt. Who can resist those pecs on display? Bart's wife, Amber, was lovely and wore Bart and Beau's grandmother's ring on her finger. It was the same ring Bart had tried to give me. I was very polite and tried not to look at it. She didn't appear concerned about me, which was definitely A-OK with me. Everyone razzed me that night about fulfilling my college dream of becoming a meteorologist and they were impressed I'd landed the big morning job at KHWB. With the Gayle Force name, Beau said laughing, "You are a Force to be reckoned with."

Everyone seemed congratulatory. As we were leaving, Beau asked me if we could meet sometime for a drink so we could catch up. Like a foolish high school girl, my heart flip-flopped. I was thrilled and practically giggled as I said, "Sure." The rest is a history of how to get dumped in three weeks. When we met at The

Fish House on The Wharf, we got to laughing about old times and Beau said he'd always had a crush on me. Somehow, we landed back at his condo in Hillsboro. Too much to drink landed us in each other's arms. It was very romantic for a few weeks, yet one day he just stopped calling. I cried when I was home at night, realizing it was over. I had checked my phone every hour for days, but I would not stoop so low as to call or text him. Then Beau called days later, fake laughing. "Hey, Gayle, I'm so sorry things got carried away between us. I just can't hurt Bart now, you know. It took him a few years to get over you. You are a beautiful, great woman and I'm sure some other guy will come along so uh...still old friends, okay, Gayle?" I was silent and so he went on. "I feel guilty. So, we'll just keep it between the two of us, okay?"

"Oh, of course," I replied keeping my voice steady but with my heart in my throat. I got off the phone quickly, feeling like an utter fool. I guess I thought he possibly had a twinge of feelings for me, but it was not the case. The crush was crushed. So, I realized the old adage was true. When he's not that into you, back off. Now back to the task at hand. I must text him and so I do.

I write: "Hey Beau, I have an urgent police question to ask you. Can we meet today or soon for a quick drink? It won't take long. Thanks! Gayle."

I put the thought of Beau texting back as an impossibility, but stay hopeful. If not, I have Plan B prepared. I have Magic's health and safety now as the most important thing to focus on.

The morning is beautiful but cooler than normal. Magic is doing well and she and Maurice are actually playing. I get dressed; no walk for me this morning. I put Magic in my Mustang and off we go down Main Street to get to Beach Tails Animal Hospital. As I wait for my vet to call us in to check the little dog over, I see Beau has texted back that he has time today at four-thirty for a quick drink before he meets his date at Pal's Captain's Inn in Hillsboro. Okay, I calm myself, I can't be embarrassed as I need to find out what to do about Doc Jeremiah. I'll be completely cool, poised, and honest. I have to.

Pal's Captain's Inn, unfortunately for two non-lovers, is the most romantic restaurant in Hillsboro, ten miles from Mystic Bay. It's a breathtaking spot with a bar overlooking the magnificence of the Pacific Ocean. Of course, Beau must be taking his date there. I mean, why else would he want to meet at a date night haven?

Arriving home, I spot Aunt Nancy and Uncle Dick getting into their car to go to the best breakfast place in the world, The Next Door Café. Uncle Dick is Mom's older brother. He didn't get the psychic gene like she did, but what he did get was the brilliant gene. He's a retired scientist. Aunt Nancy just retired from teaching history and children with special needs at Mystic Bay High. She's such a wise and caring teacher. They are surprised at meeting Magic and fall in love the second they see her. "Josh says I can keep her and if tests come out okay, she and Prince can play. Josh says she's been spayed, and no pet with her description is on any website I could find, so he chipped her and she's mine, or am I hers? She must have been dropped off near us in Mystic Bay because there are no visible sores and she's about a year old."

"How can people just drop off animals in neighborhoods?" Aunt Nancy is upset but bends down, petting Magic.

"I know. But Aunt Nancy, it seemed like a little miracle she was placed here for me. The town known for angels brought her here because I missed Lilee so much. I see an angel in dreams, like so many do in this town, so maybe the angel brought her."

"What a beautiful thought," Aunt Nancy says. "I see an angel in my dreams from time to time. Her angel face is paled by her glow, but her wings are a soft blue gray. I wish I knew her name."

"Susan," I say with ease. "Wow, it just came to me like this!" I click my fingers.

"Amazing," says Aunt Nancy. "Truly amazing! You have your mother's gift for sure. Angels are indeed here. I wish Marie and Ted would move back here."

"Me too, but Mom and Dad want to be around their new grandson, Jonny, and my stepbrother, Julian, so I get it, I really do."

"How's Maurice with Magic?" Uncle Dick loves cats but he's slightly allergic.

"Maurice loves her and they sleep together like he did with Lilee."

"Yes, Gayle, this is wonderful for her and you," says Uncle Dick picking her up. "She needs to gain some weight but she's in the best hands now!"

"We'll babysit anytime," says Aunt Nancy. Our yards are surrounded by hedges and lovely flowers. There's a little gate between the yards so we can go back and forth. My little three-bedroom stucco bungalow with a tile roof and blue door dwarfs in comparison to their red-roofed, two-story stucco with a trellis, peach-colored shutters, and window boxes galore. I feel so good living next to them. It's a family compound. I can count on them and they on me, of course. We hug goodbye and my new animal companion trots in the house, ready to find her new pal, Maurice.

...

Pal's Captain's bar is not crowded. I see Beau, looking suave, sitting at a table for two by the enormous floor-to-ceiling windows with a one eighty view. He looks good, of course, in black jeans, loafers, polo shirt, and blue blazer. He stands and gives me a peck on the cheek. He waits for me to sit down. I must have tried on most of my dresses, but I decided on the denim pant suit I love and can't wear to work. I've put my hair in the usual ponytail and wear very little make-up, which is my usual style except on the air. I wear the red pumps Maggie gave me for Christmas last year and my suede jacket. Knowing what I am about to share with Beau, I realize I should call my parents and tell them, after I know whether Beau will help me figure this whole thing out. It's my vacation in a week and I don't want to alarm them. It's then I decide I'll keep my psychic thoughts about Evelyn to myself until I can sit down and explain what's happening to my psychic mother and father in person.

After we order, the young, pretty, female, flippant server doesn't even glance at me. It's beer for him, Chardonnay for me. Beau looks at me with interest, yet no emotion I can see. It's as if the nights of wild romance never happened for him. He doesn't waste time.

"So?"

I lean in close, but the server interrupts the moment and outright flirts with Beau. She has brought the wine pronto and a house appetizer of crab dip and crackers. Since I'm allergic to shellfish, I say to her, "I'm allergic to this dip. Could we have some of those great bar nuts you serve, please?" She nods, giving me a dirty look, and walks away. I sip the wine before I speak with confidence, yet in a whisper that only he can hear.

"Well, Beau, as you may or may not remember, I have a bit of an intuitive mind."

"Yes, I remember, you seem to figure out all the police shows on TV." Beau laughs, and it sort of makes me mad.

"Well, I had a dream and ... uh ... I think Tory's boss is not taking care of her ailing husband. I think she's going to possibly do him in like the crime shows we used to watch in college. I have incredible psychic feelings about his well-being and danger." I sit back satisfied with my amateur detective speech.

Beau waits a beat before he almost shouts, "What?"

The well-dressed snooty couple two tables over both give us a furious look because he shouted, but I pay them no mind. Beau starts laughing rather loudly and then the couple really seems huffy and turn away from us. Whispering again, I say, "This is real, Beau. I have feelings. I won't say his or her name out loud, but this is happening in real time, I know it is. I was at the fundraiser the other night, saw the slides of him on the screen, and I feel it in my bones. My mind, my DREAM showed me that she's about to do harm to him, pushing him in a pool."

Beau keeps his voice low, shaking his head. "This is ridiculous, Gayle. Oh my God, foolish. You want me to what... investigate? I don't have time for this nonsense. Really! You may be a little psychic but not quite like your mother. As a young woman, she solved the biggest missing person case in San Francisco. But you are over thirty and what cases have you solved?" Beau is acting downright dismissive and mean, and he shakes his dark blonde head and downs his glass of beer. I gulp my wine and almost choke. I remain composed. I know how to keep my demeanor calm, and always have. On-the-spot weather reports and on-the-spot situations, pretending not to be hurt and aggravated at the same time are my strengths.

The flirty server plunks the nuts down on the table and gives Beau a beautiful smile before she leaves. Still keeping my voice down, I tell him, "I have notes I've written, clues." I pull a sheet of paper out of my red leopard bag and try to hand it to him, but he won't look at it.

"I'm not going to help you. You are on your own here, Gayle. You can tell, I think, this is a playing-at-detective game and dangerous too. You can't go around accusing people of something that may happen in the future. Listen, I have to go, okay?" He signals the flirty server and hands her his card. When the server leaves after a wink, he looks at me and I can tell Beau notices then the devastated look on my face.

"Look, maybe I'll ask around. I know who you're talking about. Maybe I'll be in touch but please don't do anything stupid, okay?"

I decide not to reply. I pick up the notes on the table and put them in my handbag. He signs the bar tab and leaves it on the table. I decide to get up before he does and say, "If you could check around, that would be great." Of course, I want him to follow me out and tell me he's sorry for putting me down, but he doesn't. This didn't go well at all. What a fool I was to think it would. The sea wind blows my ponytail around and though the wind has picked up, I take a breath and am glad I asked for help. It's so beautiful out. Yet, I do feel a sudden chill and wrap my arms around myself. I take in a sea breath, walk quickly to my Mustang, and take off. In my rearview mirror, I see Beau standing with his hands on his hips, looking at me drive away. I see him take out his phone. I drive fast down the hill with tears forming. What now, what next? Plan B? The angel in my dream wants me to help Doc Jeremiah. Suddenly calmer, I thank the angel for giving me the gift of intuition. I may not be my mother, Marie Russo Force, who solved the April Sorenson case twenty-eight years ago, but I am going to save Doc; I know I will.

Chapter 4

Plan B

I decide to turn back up the hill and drive north on Hillsboro Road up a little farther to the area where I know Evelyn and Doc Jeremiah live. Tory told me Doc's been homebound a month. Their home is in the most exclusive subdivision in this area, called Sailors Knot. Doc Jeremiah Parker is a nationally known cardiologist and moved to this upscale location years ago before his wife, Harriet, passed away. I drive around the posh area for a few minutes but don't know the exact address. I drive down Sea Grape Circle and feel this might be the street. There are five houses all spaced with big yards with low stone walls around them. Some have ocean views. I will ask Tory to meet with me tomorrow for breakfast at The Next Door Café. I'll tread very carefully with questions about where Evelyn and Doc live. Tory must not know what I'm doing. Then I'll ask Donnie Whitefeather, our former Chief of Police, Uncle Dick's friend, and owner of the restaurant, to help me, but I'll be vague. Donnie and his lively wife, Laurjean, own The Next Door Café, which has the best pancakes in California.

I get home to the hugs of my cat and dog. We snuggle and I go to sleep wondering if I will ever get over Beau dumping me and dismissing my intuition. It's then I feel the presence of my father, Joe. I've only seen his photos. His movie star looks and bright smile make me miss the man I'll never know on earth. Mom says I have his eyes. All I know is she loved him dearly and I was made from love. I tell him I love him in my mind and I'm sure I will sleep well knowing angels and my father are always nearby.

......

Tory and I sit by the large picture window in the ever-busy Next Door Café on Mainstreet. Laurjean Whitefeather pours our coffee and makes us laugh with her shiny outfit today of glittery pink t-shirt, matching pink jeans, and tennis shoes with pink bows. Her hair is pulled back with a rhinestone scarf. She's known for her inventive, wild clothing style. Tory and I order the Sunshine Pancakes and talk of the fundraiser and the two million dollars raised. "You did such job, Tory. Every detail was perfect. I especially loved the butterfly décor."

"Thanks for coming and doing the interviews. It was great, wasn't it? But Evelyn was mad at all of us when it was over, complaining about everything. She took me aside and was furious that you were wearing, as she said a 'cheap copy' of her dress. She accused me of telling you what she was wearing. I told her I didn't know what she was wearing to the event. Gosh, she never mentioned it. It was awful."

"Oh no, Tory. I am sorry. I thought it was funny, never thinking you'd be in trouble for that. I got that dress last minute on sale. What kind of human being is she? Not human, I'm thinking."

"You got that right." Tory tears up.

"Look Tory, listen. It'll be okay. This is her nature. Just be proud of yourself and do the job you love and ignore her, please."

"I want to, but it's hard."

I decide not to ask for specifics about Doc and Evelyn's house. I just can't, so instead I say, "Tell me about Doc Jeremiah. What illness does he have?"

"He's got dementia, she says it came on suddenly after a mini stroke. He was fine the week before. Evelyn hired a caregiver who stays most of the day with him. Doc stays in the casita in the back of the house there on Sea Grape Circle. I went there once to bring her some papers. He built it for Harriet, his late wife, who he loved dearly. She was a gem.

"What a lovely setting, with a view of the Pacific. It's up near Pal's Captain's Inn. Doc and Harriet built the Somerset Organization together. The tension between Doc and his son came to a head when he married Evelyn a few years ago. When he left the business, we all knew Evelyn's cunning ways shooed Jeremiah's son, Tyler, away from Doc. Since she's been running the business, it's all going to hell, I think. She'll ruin the place; morale is low. Doc had her in a VP position.

Her job was a fluffy non-job. But apparently, our legal department said he signed the papers for her to be CEO as he began to fail. People admire her for her looks and money, but we all fear her for her brutal nature."

"Oh Tory, this is sad. Could you think of moving on now?"

"No, I can't. I love my co-workers and contact with the population we help. We all loved Doc Jeremiah's son, Tyler. When he left, everyone resigned themselves to try to keep a strong work ethic, except now she's in charge."

Our pancakes come and I realize everything pictured in my dream might be a future reality. It is terrifying. "Does Evelyn care about Doc at all?"

"She complains about how hard it is to care for him, and she also complains about the homeless population we serve. She says they're dirty and need to move on and away from downtown. We all believe she really wants to let go of the business and spend the money."

"How did Evelyn meet Doc?" It's noisy in the restaurant and a good thing no one can hear us. Tory replies, "At a cocktail party. Doc was a wealthy established doctor and she was the sexy gold digger who worked in HR at St. Mary's where he used to do heart surgery. His vulnerability made him a target four months after he laid his wife to rest. Harriet was a dear. I started working for their project, re-designing old hotels, motels, and apartment houses to renovate for the homeless. It was idealistic, and they both shared the dream and pushed on finding staff and investors. Together, they changed so many lives. But Harriet died suddenly, and he became a broken man. Tyler worked with him but when Doc married Evelyn so soon, the relationship between father and son tanked. He did his job but the atmosphere in the office was dark." Tory says sarcastically, "Ev's a real beauty, isn't she?"

"Yes, how sad."

"When Doc fell ill so fast, we couldn't believe it."

We stop talking, realizing our pancakes are getting cold. Laurjean sashays over with her cheeriness and pours more coffee. Our conversation moves to other subjects. I'm just about as down as Tory is.

After breakfast, I take Tory over to the house to meet Magic. Tory falls in love with her, as everyone who meets her does. We make a plan to get Tory's little poodle and Magic together. As we hug goodbye at her car, Tory says, "You are a true friend and always here for me. I'm here for you too. Wish I lived closer."

"Tory, move here, it would be so fun. This town is so picturesque, and the people are nicer than most. The 'Town of Angels' people call it now."

"Maybe someday. Right now, I could use an angel."

"People here say they are everywhere. Ask your angels to help you. That's what I do." Desperate to tell Tory about my angel dream, I hold back. I can't right now.

Tory half smiles, "I need to live near my job right now. I'm on call 24/7 since she became my boss."

"What time is your workday over?" A light bulb goes on in my brain, but obviously I don't tell Tory.

"We all leave at five. Evelyn insists on it as she likes to go out each night of the week now that Doc is ill."

"Where does she go?"

"To bars, mostly. She gets all dressed up before she leaves work and puts on even more make-up, if possible. She mentions Nick's Catch in North Beach mostly. I've never been there but it's supposed to have fabulous food. She also goes to The Bayview Club."

"Let's go to both sometime and check them out," I say with tongue in cheek.

"No way, I don't want to be caught going there and her seeing me. It's too risky and scary."

"Do you think she is taking good care of Doc at all?"

"No way. I feel awful about it. No love there."

"Well, don't you think someone should report it? Could you or someone talk to Tyler Parker about it?"

"Oh no, that woman is a snake. Who knows what she'd do if she found out any of us were tattling on her." As Tory leaves and I wave goodbye, I can't help feeling sorry for her. I've always loved the jobs I've had. Even the server job during college with Tory at Stone Creek Golf Club. I can't imagine working for a slimy female potential murderer like Evelyn Parker. Now, I really have the chills and I'm wearing a down jacket.

Chapter 5
The Intuitive Detective

Before I left the restaurant, I asked Laurjean and Donnie if I can come over to the restaurant and talk after they close this afternoon. They agreed. I'm sure they wonder what I want to speak to them about. Main Street is bustling on this Sunday in June, with bright flower baskets swinging in the cool breeze on the posts down Main Street and the tourists and townsfolk are all smiles. The sea air lightly touches my face. I live in California's most charming town. I run into Maggie taking her walk. We chat briefly and I tell her about Magic, and we decide to meet Thursday for tea at the Tea and Tarot Shop. I explain I'll be going to see my parents in San Diego on Friday.

Walking into the restaurant, the smell of breakfast cooking still permeates the air. Donnie, a big Native American, comes out of the kitchen and smiling Laurjean has the pot of coffee on the table. She locks the door and we sit in the corner. It's funny to be here after the rush this morning. There is still the sound of clanging dishes washing in the back as the staff finishes up for the day.

Donnie starts, "So, Gayle, tell us what's going on? Everyone good?"

"Yes, yes of course. Um, well, this is a police question. Since you were the chief for a long time here, I know I can trust you. But please, can I ask you to keep it between us just for a little while? I need your advice."

Laurjean looks at Donnie with an expression I can't read and before he can speak, she says, "Gayle, we're worried, so please tell us what is going on."

"You know I'm a smidgeon psychic. It's in my blood, like my mom and late grandmother. I had a dream about something criminal that might happen soon. I don't want to tell you right now because it may be just a bad dream but an angel who I see in my dreams showed me a scenario taking place in the future and she wants me to help."

They both look at each other. "Can you tell us what you are seeing?"

"I don't want to upset you but it's possibly physical harm to someone."

"Oh my," says Laurjean. Her hand reaches out to mine.

Donnie says, "Gayle, is it someone you know?"

"No, not personally, but I recognize him. He's ill and has a business in San Francisco. I asked an old college friend who's a detective in the San Francisco Police Department to help me and he laughed it off, saying I was crazy with all this psychic stuff. But you two know psychics have abilities here in town and I have a slight ability. The angel I see came to me Thursday night and showed me what will be occurring in the future and the person I need to help. Later that evening, I was astonished when I saw the man in a photograph at an event. I've never seen the future before, but it looks like someone is going to hurt him in the future. It's not a coincidence."

Donnie says, "Listen Gayle, I know a guy who works with the San Francisco Police Department on occasion. His late father was a friend of mine in law enforcement. His name is Alex Knight. He is an immigration attorney but has helped the police with his intuition. He helped find a missing baby in a case similar to your mother's that she solved long ago. Alex kept it totally under the radar this time, as he knew that your mother found out the notoriety was hard, which is why your parents left town. When a psychic's name is in the news, the media jump on it. Alex helped solve the missing child case, and others, and does keep a low profile. Would you consider talking to him first? He would understand and help before we go to Chief Peter Warren of the San Francisco police? I say this because I want to be involved and if this is a real potential crime, then we have to go to the police."

I explain, "The detective I talked to was Beau Bolton, and he just blew me off. If Alex Knight can help me figure this out, I'd be so appreciative. You both don't think I'm crazy, do you?"

"No, Gayle," Donnie assures me. "You have the ability. It's been passed on to you and you must follow through. We believe you and we will help in any way we can."

"I can't believe how wonderful you two are. Thank you. I will contact him."

"Let me call him. If I get him, you can talk to him now. I remember how your mother, Marie, solved the April Sorenson missing child case years ago. She shied away from everyone after that. Her name was in the paper, and you were so small; she felt she and Ted had to protect you and leave the San Francisco area. She left Mystic Bay and we all were sad for that."

"I know but here I am, and it's been so long now. She helps the San Diego police sometimes and she's glad she kept the house for me. I just want to help this man if this is really real."

Laurjean says in a quiet voice, "It's real, Gayle. Don't doubt your intuition. Look at all the people in town who have abilities. Our old wonderful late psychic, Madam Norma, put this town on the map. She showed the world psychic abilities are a normal part of many lives. She was respected and revered. She helped so many. Now Maggie has taken her place as the most respected psychic in town. Are you going to share this with her? I know you are best friends."

"Yes, I will tell her some of it. We are meeting this week for tea."

"Good, she'll help too. Maggie wanted to be anonymous for years, but then I'm sure the reason she came forward was to help people. You know your mother helped solve so many crimes too while living in San Francisco. But then she went underground with her gift."

I'm so glad I came to them and feel some relief. Donnie says, "Let me see if I can get ahold of Alex now." He walks away from us and moves to the front of restaurant, looking out the window as he calls. I hear a few words in the conversation but Laurjean talks to me, her words soothing.

"You are doing the right thing, Gayle. Intuition is part of the energy of the town. Look at all the volunteering and love that this town gives to others. It's a blessed place where angels appeared to children a few years back. I know you know

Maggie was there when the child with special needs saw an angel. Our town is a place of peace and love, harmony and giving. Isn't it wonderful?"

"Oh yes, Laurjean. Have you ever had psychic or angel experience?"

"Well, I 'm not psychic but Madam Norma counselled me once. When I was in college, I had such an urge to go to North Dakota and study my very small bit of Sioux heritage. Madam Norma knew I'd meet the love of my life while there and advised me to go straight away. The love of my life, of course, was Donnie. He's an angel on earth."

"How wonderful. Yes, I do feel a little scared, but I think I've been suppressing these feelings all my life. Not following my gut, my intuition, so many times, I guess. But please promise you won't share this with my aunt or uncle yet. I can't worry anyone, especially them. I'll tell my mom and dad this coming weekend when I go to San Diego. Mom may have some intuition ideas of her own."

Donnie brings his cell to me. "I have Alex on the line." I take the phone. "Hello, this is Gayle Force." He sounds pleasant with a deep voice. I tell him I'm in need of a person who can advise me with a psychic dream about a future crime and he replies, "Of course, I have had experience. Any friend of Donnie and a Laurjean's is a friend of mine."

We agree to meet at The Half Time Grill by the football stadium tomorrow, Monday, at 6:30 pm. I get a good feeling about him. As I leave the Next Door Café, I thank Donnie and Laurjean with hugs and reassurance that I will be careful. I walk to my house on the corner of Cove Lane and Sea Breeze Road. I ponder what is next for amateur me. Am I crazy or am I becoming the very psychic my mother is?

On Main Street, I notice the happy Sunday crowds. The sun is shining and the sight of the harbor is glorious when I get to my house. I can see the harbor just a little walk from my front yard. It's breathtaking with so many boats; too many to count. Maurice always runs out of the cat door to greet me. He curls around my legs and Magic, who can't get out the small cat door, is waiting for me inside by the door. Their happiness at seeing me is all I need.

I think about Beau. If I tell him, "Oh, never mind, I have a psychic detective on the case as of tomorrow," I fear he will laugh. But real fear creeps in. Will Alex Knight truly believe I've seen a futuristic event? Will he want to help me? I feel the whisper of my angel in my mind: "All will be well, your heart knows."

After going outside with Magic, I decide to eat leftovers sitting on the couch with a dog and cat nestled on either side. I turn on the TV to the recording of my interview at the event for Somerset House.

Oh my gosh, I do a pretty good job, I think, dressed like Evelyn to boot, but there is a moment when I spy the evil Evelyn in the corner at the back of the scene, peering from behind a door at my interview! I immediately call Tory. "You won't believe this!" When I've told her, she says, "Evelyn is so competitive. She couldn't stand it that you had that dress on."

"I'm sorry. I tell you all the time you don't deserve this treatment. Look, I feel so sorry for Doc Jeremiah."

I know I shouldn't have brought it up again, but I had to. She stuns me with her answer: "I think he's taken care of minimally. She keeps him in the casita behind her house with an older caregiver. He has a doctor who comes in occasionally. I think Doc is all alone at night. Since Tyler isn't at work anymore, nobody knows what is going on. No one talks about it at work because they are too afraid of her to discuss it. No gossip. But he used to be so robust and larger than life a month ago. When asked about him, she blows people off. 'It's so hard being a care giver,' she complains. No love there, she's a woman with no heart!"

We talk some more about it, but when we hang up, I close my eyes in prayer. I will tell Alex Knight all I know and see what he says. My mission is to help the vulnerable, ailing Dr. Jeremiah Parker, philanthropist, good doctor, and too good for the heartless Evelyn Parker.

My attention turns to Magic. It's funny, the dog is staring, watching me on TV. She seems to know it's me on the screen. This gives me an incredible idea. I find it's helpful to think of something else for a moment besides poor Doc Parker.

It's Monday on *Good Morning San Francisco*. I'm dressed in my red skirt, black top, and red checked jacket. As I cheerily bring the weather forecast to the viewers, I have fun with it, "Across the country today it's hot hot hot! Look, the east is having a doozy of a June with upper ninety degrees from Maine to Florida. Whew! The southwest is parched dry and over one hundred today. Here in the Bay Area, well, our regular summer chill is getting a bit of a warmup after noon. Max breezes today, warming up to sixty-five, so everyone, do keep your fuzzy slippers and bathrobe on this morning, have some more coffee. You'll need to take a jacket today for sure. Don't forget the sunscreen. But tomorrow the wind will be blowing and the cooler weather will be upon us, low sixties but sunny skies. Tonight will be a gorgeous starry night with meteor showers after midnight, and that's why I'm wearing my star earrings! Coming up Friday morning, Mark and Jeni, I have two surprises for you all, but it's a secret. Our boss, Wes, said yes to them both so you viewers just have to wait four days to find out!"

"We know, Gayle. They don't call you Gayle Force for nothing," laughs anchor Mark.

"Can't wait," laughs Jeni, who reports traffic.

......

I've been thinking all day about my two plans. My vet, Josh, calls and says Magic's blood work came out just fine so I can take her to Dog Beach and she can play with Prince. When I come home, both dog and cat are cozying up to each other on the blue couch with five pillows, watching TV. It's so cute. I leave my TV on and recorded so every weekday morning my animals can watch me on my show. I have my bagel and cream cheese with herbs for a late lunch and start preparing for not only my meeting with Alex Knight but the other plan which came flooding in while I watched the moon last night. I go into the closet to figure out what to wear before taking Magic over to meet Prince, and then on we'll go to Dog Beach for fun and a walk. I pick out the San Francisco Shakers Jersey, jacket, and hat to meet Alex. We both shared what we would wear so we'd recognize each other. He'll be wearing the same thing. Of course, so will most of the people there as it's a big place for Shaker fans. He'll be in the right corner in a red leather booth with a mug of beer, and he told me he has a short brown beard.

Up on the top shelf, I get out the box with the brown wig I wore to a costume party last year. I came as Lois Lane to my date's Superman. I find my brown faux leather jacket that doesn't fit right that I bought mistakenly on sale after Christmas long ago. This is what I'll wear to scope out Nick's Catch before I meet Alex. Maybe it's stupid but I have an intuitive hunch that Evelyn Parker will be there. Even if I'm wrong, I'll get a sense of the population that frequent the bar and restaurant. According to the website, there's a separate bar with fish and Italian appetizers. The main menu is fancier with fish, Italian dishes with meat and fish dishes along with steaks and salads. It all looks really delicious.

Our meet and greet with Prince goes swimmingly. They are pals and so off we go to Dog Beach. It's here where I find my happy place, the most dog-friendly and people-friendly place on earth. It's a magical place to me. I feel the energy of the earth, sea, and residents the moment each time I drive over the town line, just as I did as a child every precious summer.

It's time. I drive into the parking lot behind Nick's Catch. As I get out of my car and walk to the front, I note the restaurant is in a quaint old building of the 1920s or so. It has a red door and the smell of a mixture of delicious foods waft in the air as I walk into the bar. A few eyes turn and look at me then turn back. I have made myself look as plain as possible, frumpy coat with a brown, uninteresting hair wig to my shoulders and no make-up, only light pink lip gloss. But then I spot her. Evil Ev sits at the bar with her profile toward me, talking and laughing with all the older men at the bar. She does look good though, long legs crossed, wearing black slacks and a low shocking pink cowl sweater. Her black jacket lies across the back of the bar stool. Her make-up is thick, and she would be pretty to me if I didn't know the meanness that runs through her being. A young woman takes me to a little table by the window where I can see her clearly. She doesn't look my way. A dark-haired young and unsmiling server wearing a black shirt and pants and red tie walks up to me. In monotone, he says, "I'm Guiseppi. Can I start you with a glass of wine?" He still doesn't smile.

"Yes, Guiseppi, I love your name. I'll have your house Chardonnay if you have one, please."

"It's from Washington and not very good. Our Italian wine called Balducci is better."

"Oh, Guiseppi, thank you, I am part Italian, but I think I'll stick with the Chard from Washington. I love that one."

Guiseppi gives me a one-eyebrow look with a smirk, doesn't speak, and leaves. I wonder how I made him mad. Maybe I said his name too many times, I guess. I turn to watch Evelyn put on a show, carried away laughing at some non-joke. Then a very handsome, fiftyish, Italian-looking man walks in from the kitchen, dressed in a well-tailored black suit and open white shirt revealing a lot of chest hair and gold chains. Evelyn becomes flustered and as he kisses her cheek, and my slightly psychic radar goes haywire. She's in love with him! That's why she comes here! Guiseppi returns.

With a dour expression, he asks, "Would you like an appetizer? The fried mozzarella ARE what most people order."

"Sounds good, Guiseppi," I say like a happy cheerleader at homecoming. I can feel my wig slip a little but I don't want to touch it. He looks at me for a stare down for a moment but then leaves. Evelyn's laugh could break the sound barrier. It's Cruella, only worse. She glances my way but appears to see right through me. The bar is becoming crowded now with couples and singles, mostly older. The food coming to other tables by Guiseppi and another server looks and smells so good. Mini pizzas, sourdough rolls, crab cakes, crab legs and steaks on skewers. Beers, wine, and martinis are everywhere. The crowd is upscale. My mozzarella comes and Guiseppi plunks it down on the table without a word. I decide to continue as Miss Congeniality: "Thanks, dear Guiseppi." He looks displeased. Uh oh, that gorgeous Italian man is walking up to tables saying hello and he's coming toward my table next. I squirm in my seat as he approaches. "Hello, my dear, welcome. I haven't seen you here before. Am I correct? I'm Nick, the owner of the restaurant. Are you enjoying your mozzarella? It's my favorite for sure."

"It's really delicious," I say with a smile.

"Is this your first time here?" Nick offers me an engaging smile.

"Why, yes. It's wonderful, thank you," I say with a mouthful.

"What's your name, dear," Nick asks sincerely. I quickly think as I swallow and say my middle name, which is my mother's name.

"Marie."

"Tell me why a pretty Marie like you is here alone?"

I lie the lie I have to: "Oh, I'm meeting a date after this. I just wanted to try a little appetizer before I met him. It's a blind date and I want to have some food in my stomach, just in case." I wink and give him a bigger smile as my wig seems to tilt more. Hope gorgeous Nick can't tell.

"How charming and funny you are. If he's not the one, you come back here, okay? I'll have the kitchen fix you a delicious crab dinner!"

I can't tell him I'm allergic to crab, so I say, "I will, thank you, Nick. How nice of you." He leaves and I stuff my face with the rest of the mozzarella and finish my wine. I've got to get out of here. Also, I catch Evelyn staring at Nick as he wanders from table to table chatting. Did she look at me while I was talking with Nick? Yikes! I call Guiseppi over, which doesn't make him happy, asking for my check. Evelyn speaks to Nick again as he walks up to her. She smiles sweetly with those fangs of hers and suddenly I see a snake face. I shake my head. What's happening to the "weather girl" in me? I am definitely becoming a psychic detective! Evelyn kisses Nick on the cheek and starts to put her coat on. I decide to follow her out from a distance.

Guiseppi brings me the bill and I pay in cash as quickly as I can. Giving him a large tip and a smile, I say, "Thanks for the great suggestion, Guiseppi." He doesn't speak and has a weird look in his eyes. Unfazed, I leave after Evelyn does but not too close. She gets into her black Mercedes S 550 and speeds away. I note her license plate and memorize it. It's easy. It reads Docswife1. How sad is that because Doc adored his first wife, Harriet, according to Tory. Oh, I realize it's probably Harriet's car! Focusing on my next stop, its time anyway for me to meet Alex Knight. As I drive the few blocks to The Half Time Grill, I think this is dangerously fun being a detective. But a pang in my heart turns my attention back to Doc Jeremiah in the dream. It's coming together like an ugly Halloween puzzle. Maybe the intuitive PI, Alex Knight, will help me now that I've found out about Evelyn Parker and her boyfriend or is he a crush, the handsome Italian, Nick?

Chapter 6
The Half Time Grill

Alex Knight is indeed waiting for me in the red leather corner booth. He's bearded, all right, but his blue eyes stare into mine. They have a twinkle in them, a light. He is tall and nice looking, about forty, I'm guessing. We have look-alike clothes on. I took the wig and ugly jacket off in the car and put my ponytail up in the Shaker cap. He spots me and beckons me over. There is nothing to trip over on the floor, but I manage to trip but catch myself. He stands and meets me at the edge of the table.

"It's nice to meet you, Gayle. Please sit down." We shake hands and his handshake is firm like mine. I sit down and find I can hardly speak. He's pretty easy on the eyes, as my Aunt Nancy always says about good looking men. But I relax when we start talking because he also has an easy-going demeanor too. I feel comfortable, like I've known him a long time.

Alex smiles, "I watched your morning show today. You bring so much light and fun reporting the weather. You're a natural."

Almost speechless, I reply, "Thank you."

"What would like to drink?"

"Arnold Palmer, please. I just had a glass of wine and some food."

"Would you like to eat something? Best hamburgers, grilled cheese, fish sandwiches, and salads in town. We have lots of nonalcoholic choices, too. I'm drinking one of the latest beers."

"Thanks, but I'm addicted to Arnold Palmers and French fries." Alex Knight laughs and I can tell his smile is genuine as he tells me, "You are funny."

"Not all the time," I smile.

"Bear," he shouts to the bartender. "Order the lady an Arnold and some French fries and I'll have the Half Time Vegie Burger Plate."

"Yes, Boss."

"Is this your restaurant?"

"I own a tiny piece of it, yes. I'm an attorney, as you know, but this is my place to eat a couple of nights a week. My condo is down the street. This is my second home. Now let's talk about you. You have intuition and Donnie says you've seen a potential crime in your mind?"

I start slowly telling Alex everything I told Beau and more. Alex says he's worked with people living at Somerset House and met Dr. Jeremiah Parker a year ago. He's worked with some of the homeless population on their immigration issues. It's easy spilling the whole story to Alex. "I met with an old friend from college who's now a San Francisco Police detective. I told him my dream and asked if he could help me. He blew me off."

"Really? Do you mind telling me his name?"

"Beau Bolton."

"Oh yes, I know the guy."

"Why would Beau blow me off like that? It's a future crime I saw." Of course, I don't tell Alex Beau and I had a brief romantic episode.

"Gayle, I don't say unkind things about people, though he should have guessed you did indeed need advice here."

"Beau said maybe, just maybe, he'd check but really, I think he just tried to shake me off. But there's more," I reply.

Then I tell them the big news.

"My friend Tory told me two bars Evelyn frequents, so I went to one before I came here. There she sat at the bar and flirted with all the men, and then a man I surmise is her boyfriend came in. His name is Nick, and he owns the restaurant, Nick's Catch." Alex looks at me intensely. It's a good thing it's noisy in the restaurant and no one is in the next booth as he says, "Gayle, you can't go in there again, please. He's Nick Carmeletti, known to have ties with organized crime. The FBI is aware he's been involved in drug distribution, but they are not able to make a case.

Frightened now, I say, "Wow, this is troubling, and I will stay away for sure." Our food comes and I take a drink and feel suddenly wanting to bolt. Organized crime? Alex seems to notice my anxiety. "I don't mean to scare you but perhaps we should let the police handle this premonition of yours, or the FBI."

"Alex, you just met me, I know. But I have this intuition like you do. I don't think it's a good idea yet. Something tells me it will be the two of us who will help Doc. I don't trust anyone but you and Donnie."

"Okay, let's make a plan for now. I'll check out Evelyn's past. You, stay away from her though, okay?"

"Yes, I will. I leave Friday for San Diego to see my family. I was planning on a week but I'm cutting it short. I will be worrying too much about Doc. But you'll keep in touch with me?"

"Of course, every day. Now let's eat and we'll figure out the rest."

"I think best when I'm eating." He laughs and I smile but I realize as I start gobbling the fries that this is dangerous territory for a person like me. What is a fun-loving meteorologist doing with my life, trying to stop a potential crime I saw in a psychic angel dream? Most folks would think I'm crazy. But the townspeople of Mystic Bay would think me just like my mother, a psychic trying to right a wrong, helping someone I've never met.

I sip my drink. What if I have another dream? My intuition alerts me that pushing Doc Jeremiah in the pool is just in the planning stage. When we are finished, I explain everything I'm thinking.

I tell him of Tory's opinion about how Evelyn treats her at work. I explain I was discreet, but I asked her if she felt Doc is in harm's way and Tory's impression told me more. "I think it's all in the planning stage so what else can I do if you are doing the detective work?"

"Just don't say anything else to Tory; she may not be trustworthy is what I'm getting."

I'm shocked at what he's saying. "I've known her since I was eighteen. Why do you think that?"

"It's the hunch, the intuition, Gayle. I know you are wondering why I don't use the word psychic?"

"It's just a word."

"People think psychic has a negative connotation, but it doesn't. I prefer using the words sensitive or intuitive."

"But Alex, in Mystic Bay, where I live there, are many psychics and it's a lovely town and people come from all over to experience the kindness of people, the vibe. Angels were spotted by little children in our town and my husband's friend filmed a documentary about the sightings. He wrote a book about it too. There's a bestselling book written about the life of our famous late psychic Madam Norma. She saw angels everywhere."

"I know, it's a special place. I love The Next Door Café. Laurjean and Donnie have told me so much about the town, known as the 'Town of Angels.' It is indeed a magical place, really. I wish I could move there myself, but I need to be close to my work right now. I keep my intuition low-key. I was razzed by some of the San Francisco Police, guys of course. I solved two cases they couldn't figure out. It was uncomfortable, but I used my intuition and found the answers that solved the cases."

"Oh, I suppose Beau Bolton was part of that."

"Yes," Alex half smiles. "But I don't care. I have to do what I have do to help people."

"Alex, this is a business deal. I really need to pay you for your help, please. I appreciate this so much."

"No, Gayle. Thanks so much, but my work with my intuition is always pro bono. But you are sweet."

"I have to do something, please."

"Just be your nice self and keep thinking. Let me know immediately if you have another dream or intuitive hunch. Now, I know you have notes in your purse, so pull them out and let me take a look."

Wow, this guy really is psychic, I mean intuitive. I glance down at his hands. He has a wedding ring on his right hand. Married possibly, although it's the wrong hand. I won't ask about his personal life. This is business. It's detective work we're doing.

When our meeting is over, Alex insists on walking me to my Mustang and says he's a great lover of the car. "There's mine," he gestures. "There it is, the sweetest yellow Mustang ever. It's a Cobra. I call her Buttercup."

"I wish I had a name for mine like 'Red Flash' or something." We both laugh. It's nice to be with a man who's affable and kind too. Being with him tonight was as comfy as trying on an old shoe, as my mother would say. We are working together now. I have a partner in crime now, or about a crime, I guess. Sighing on the drive home, I say out loud,. "Thank you, Angel, for bringing Alex Knight my way."

Chapter 7

The Bay View Club

It's Tuesday and I've had a very busy day at work and a wonderful late afternoon with Magic at Dog Beach, yet I'm ready for detective work. I wear black jeans and a yellow turtleneck with a black coat because it's cold. There's some mist as I drive to Bay View Club. I don't think Evelyn will be there tonight. But Alex did tell me to stay away from her. He asked me to stay away from Nick's Catch and not follow her. I just want to check out The Bayview Club she goes to frequently. Am I wrong? I've got to get some clues. I blew my hair out long. No ponytail tonight. I don't want to be recognized by anyone. The public is starting to notice me while I'm out. Some come up to me, I think, because of my signature ponytail. That never happened in San Diego.

I drive up to the restaurant housed in a pretty Victorian house with a wrap-around porch. The sea mist is thick as I park and walk into the bar area. It's crowded and there are a few spots at the bar, so I sit down on an antique bar stool. The not-smiling female bartender comes over. "What will it be, miss?"

"Your house Chardonnay, please." I'm smiling at her but she doesn't return it. Okay, it's unhappy server and bartender week, I guess. I see her name is Cece. "Cece, I'd love some sour dough bread and butter too, and please do charge me for it."

"Don't worry, miss. I will charge you." Man, is she being sarcastic?

Why am I annoying to wait staff? Oh well, I'm always an excellent tipper.

Oh no, there he is again! Nick Carmeletti walks by but doesn't notice me. Of course, I look different -- no brown wig. I put my head down a little then look at him walk into the restaurant area. Nick's dressed in a very expensive suit and tie. Yikes again, there I see Evelyn Parker in a short black leather skirt and off the shoulder silver top at a table by a window. He walks up to her with a kiss on the cheek. He must own both restaurants. I can't look at them, but thankfully my glass of wine comes with the bread. Everyone at the bar is talking to their neighbor and so I devour the bread, slathering it with butter like I've been on a no-carb diet for too long. Alex told me not to follow her. But I didn't follow her! I wouldn't have and I never guessed she'd be coming in here and that her boyfriend Nick would own this place too! Oh gosh! Where was my intuition this time? "Eat, drink, and run," I whisper to myself.

I can see Nick and Evelyn through the bar mirror in front of me, though. Evelyn looks good as always. She has her hair in the typical chignon. Her tight face lift is beaming. Her clothes and expensive shoes make me notice she must have quite a clothing allowance. Champagne is served immediately to them, and I glance down at my plate. I've stuffed in every bit of butter and bread I could in ten seconds. Nothing like San Francisco sourdough. I decide to finish my wine slowly and then walk out slowly. I have to drive home and figure out this scenario. I don't look again at them in the mirror. I hear Evelyn's loud, annoying laugh; it makes me certain Evelyn is having an affair with Nick Carmeletti while her poor husband ails at home. Let's face it. What's happening to me is not good. I'm caught up in a mess I don't even know is real. It's from a dream.

"More bread?" The bartender still acts perturbed, but I say politely, "No thanks, Cece." I smile a fake smile at her and she slaps the bill on the table. Then suddenly a thought, a message that I'm sure is from my angel comes to me: "You are doing everything you can."

I get a tap on my shoulder. I turn quickly. It's Alex Knight! He looks handsome and his hair is wavy and light brown like his beard. His eyes twinkle and he wears a black sweater like mine. I can't speak.

"Hi honey, time to go now." He then puts too much cash down on the bill. The seat next to me is empty but Alex doesn't sit down and he doesn't look angry. Does he know Evelyn's here? Does he think I followed her? By the way, why is he here?

He helps me put my coat on and we leave away from Evelyn, who I don't look at. We walk out into the cool night. Then, as we walk to my car, Alex says, "Gayle, I know you didn't follow Evelyn, but why go to restaurants you know she goes to?"

"I just wanted to get the feel of the place. I'm sorry. I didn't see her car. I didn't know Nick owned this place too."

"He doesn't. That's Gino, his twin brother. He's not in organized crime. Never has been. He's rejected the family but won't give the FBI any information. He's a legit owner of the restaurant. He told the FBI that in his late mother's honor he will say nothing against any of the family."

"I can't believe Nick has a twin and Evelyn is being courted by brothers. Or is she courting them?"

"I would say, Gayle, that she's the pursuer. But please go home. I'm doing some research and you and I can meet Thursday night to discuss them. I'll come over to your place around 5:30. Is that okay? I want to stop and see Donnie and Laurjean too."

"Of course. My address is 525 Cove Lane." Alex stops walking to put the information into his phone.

"I'll make you spaghetti, okay?"

"Are you sure? How nice of you. Thank you! I'll call you tomorrow if anything comes up." It's then we see Evelyn coming out of the restaurant. She and Gino are arguing but I can't make out what they are saying. Then we hear in a loud voice, "Evie, don't leave," Again Gino calls after her as she stomps towards the parking area. It's too late for us to flee so Alex pulls me close. He whispers, "Bury your face in my jacket." He puts his arms around me and I do the same to him. I have my face against his chest and man, do I feel safe. Alex buries his face in my hair away from Evelyn's gaze. Oh my God, is this really happening? He's prevented Evelyn from seeing our faces.

I hear the fast clip clop of her heels as she walks by. "Get a room," Evelyn says in a throaty, angry whine. We just keep on holding each other. We hear her get into her car and the car start. We get up for air when we hear her drive away. In the misty night, I look up at him as we pull apart. His face is smiling but he says seriously, "A close one. Too close, Miss Gayle Force. Now do you see my point. She can't see either of our faces anywhere she goes."

I'm feeling discombobulated. "This time I didn't get a feeling Evelyn would be here. Yes, I get it, your point. But what kind of person yells at strangers hugging? She's bizarre at best."

"I know. Please, Gayle, don't go anywhere she goes from now on. Leave the sleuthing to me."

"Alex, I promise Thank you for coming to my aid here."

"I'll call you tomorrow if, hopefully, I get some answers to my leads."

"Okay, thanks again."

We say our goodbyes and get into our Mustangs. I see him behind me turning on the road that leads to the highway. I want to drive by Evelyn and Doc's house on Sea Grape Circle on the way home through Hillsboro, but I don't. As I drive home in the night, my mind turns to Alex. Such quick thinking. I forgot to tell him I was utterly amazed that he knew he would find Evelyn and me at the restaurant. He must be some psychic. I mean, he must be some intuitive detective!

Chapter 8
Maggie's Intuition

It's two o'clock Wednesday and my workday is done. I change into jeans and sweatshirt, take Magic, and off we walk to Main Street. Maggie Greenstreet and I sit on the heated patio of Tea and Tarot having cups of English Breakfast tea and scones. Her adorable two-month-old baby, Marshall, is in the stroller. The charming tea store where Tarot cards are read and lovely teas and pastries are served, has a peaceful, calming atmosphere like no other. Aunt Nancy and everyone I know here in town adore this place too.

Maggie and I were summer friends for years and people always thought we were sisters. Her hair is blonder than mine, but we do look similar. As our conversation moves along, Maggie says with concern, "I'm worried about you, Gayle. Something is up, right? Your eyes have a look of, well, worry."

Maggie is a known psychic now and let it be known that she has been seeing some angels near us all, just as her great grandmother did before her. She's also known for feeling the emotions of trees and nature.

"Yes, some worries, but Maggie, it's something an angel showed me in a dream. I'm trying to help someone in trouble who may be in harm's way."

"I see someone is helping you and that's good. You don't have to tell me more but do remember to reach out to me if you need to."

I look at her sweet baby, Marshall, smiling, then back at her. "You are so dear, and I appreciate your thoughtfulness. Noah and Marshall are so lucky to have you in their lives."

"Thank you, friend. You know Magic came to you by an angel's way. I'm sure of it. I'm also sure that you are in good hands, angel-wise and otherwise. This someone who is helping you is a good person and psychic. It is good."

I'm quite shocked. Does she see Alex Knight? I remain composed, "Yes, he is."

"Thought so," Maggie says, smiling while pouring us more tea. We talk some more, eating our scones. Sweet little Magic rests her furry head on my sneakers.

"Oh, by the way, Noah has a guy he wants to set you up with. I will not reveal his name because you will look him up on the internet."

Surprised, I laugh, "Is he tall, dark and handsome?" I tease her, for that would describe her husband perfectly.

"I don't know," she laughs. "I met him once. He seems like a nice guy. Noah says it's a match made in heaven!"

"Sure, how sweet of you. I'll go, but can you wait a while because Friday I will be going to San Diego to see my family for a few days."

"That's great! I'm thrilled. You need a diversion from thinking about Beau." I haven't told Maggie I met with Beau again. I wonder if her intuition has suspected as much.

"Noah and I thought we'd go to dinner at Pal's Captain's Inn, the most romantic place around." She was delighted with herself, but I decide to tell her truthfully that I'd rather go somewhere other than Pal's, really: "I had a chilly encounter, drinks with Beau there recently. He was really rude."

"Oh, did he say he was sorry for being a total fool for acting like nothing happened between you two?"

"No, no apology, just rudeness."

Maggie shakes her head. "Yes, we all kiss a frog or two, Gayle. As you know, I did so myself. Let me think, how about we go to Jack's by The Sea here in town? I haven't been there in a while. I need to go there to look out those huge windows at the spectacular setting and view, the beauty of the ocean, and of course, I love the apple torte."

"Apple torte? I love that! Yes, Maggie, it sounds lovely."

"You want the recipe? I have it from my years working there. It's easier than apple pie."

"It is apple pie," I laugh and so does she. It's wonderful to be with her and I wonder who this guy will be. I've gone on a few blind dates that end up -- well, let's say, dull at best, but if Maggie says Noah likes him ...

"Thank you for thinking of me. You are always so thoughtful."

We finish our tea and time together and we hug goodbye. I tell her I think Marshall is the most beautiful baby I've ever seen, and I'm not lying. Maggie is happier than I've ever seen her, too. I stroll home, stopping at the store to get some apples. I'll make Alex an apple torte. Walking up to my house, I find Maurice zipping up to me from the cat door and winding himself around my legs. Magic has been so good. Nothing to fix. What a little doll. When she looks at me with those brown eyes of hers, I see a sparkle as in all of the animals I've known. The look is pure love and devotion. Maurice is so happy to have a pal.

Evening comes and I've prepared for Alex coming over tomorrow night. The apple torte is out of the oven, and it smells just as great as in the restaurant. I have a slice, nice and hot. I put the rest in the fridge. I've washed my hair and dried it for tomorrow, so I lay my clothes out for my job like I always do and get on my black sheep pj's. I think of Alex coming over and having spaghetti and about the long denim shirt and jeans I'll wear, my favorite at-home style. Wrapping the throw around me, I sit on the patio for a moment with the animals snuggled near and gaze at the sky. I close my eyes in prayer for Doc. I feel my father near for a moment. His spirit always comforts me. Then the thought comes through to me that Doc's okay for now but soon he will need Alex and me. I have a vision of a woman holding the old man's hand. Then the vision leaves as quickly as it came. It's unsettling to think about Doc being neglected but I remember Maggie said it will all work out. I know that angels are calling me to help. I walk inside and my cell rings as I am preparing for bed. I know it's Alex. Maurice and Magic are snug in their bed, and I answer, plopping down on all my purple covers.

"Alex, hello, how are you?"

"Good, good. You weren't asleep yet, were you? I know you've got to go to bed early."

"No, I'm up. I usually try to be asleep by eight, no later, on work nights, but I'm just fine. Have you found out anything?"

"Yes, Gayle, your intuition was right on." I sit up in bed. "Tell me, please," I say.

"Listen to this. Evelyn Wuzneski Mellon Smithfield Parker has been married three times. She was engaged to Nick Carmeletti, right after they graduated from the same high school in Chicago!"

"Really!"

"Yes. She lived with her mother, who was a maid for the Baxter Mellon family in wealthy Lakeville, Illinois, near Chicago. The engagement was broken, I'm assuming by Nick or his family. She immediately married Baxter Mellon, Jr. She was married to him for a year, then dumped him and married a doctor named Jerry Smithfield. She worked in hospitals in HR. That marriage also ended in divorce two years later. For years, she lived in Chicago, but she moved to San Francisco the exact month Nick did four years ago. Here's the clincher. She started dating Doc Parker three years ago. She worked at St. Mary's Hospital and met the lonely widower, Doc, at a fundraiser for the hospital. His wife, Harriet, had died four months before. Next thing I found out is that Doc took her to a wealthy Somerset House patron's garden party. After dinner, Evelyn excused herself to go to the powder room. She then snuck into the master bathroom and was caught by Everett and Dixie Pomeroy, the homeowners, opening a jewelry case and putting the woman's diamond bracelet and ring into her handbag. Apparently, Evelyn begged them not to call the police, but they did. Doc Jeremiah handled it, all in the master bathroom. The party went on, but the police came after it was over, and the other guests never knew. Evelyn, of course, had given the diamonds back but I found a record of the incident because I am close friends with a San Francisco judge."

"Oh wow, Alex. This is wild."

"There's more. She and Doc flew to Las Vegas and married the next day. He lawyered her up, and no charges were made by the family. News of her stealing the jewels was squashed. Then, immediately, Doc took Evelyn into the business as his assistant at Somerset House and the rest is history."

"Alex this is insane. She's a thief and has been with Nick for years. I'm sure there is much more intrigue here."

"I know, I actually wished we didn't find anything negative that would implicate her in a crime, and yet I knew we would. Now, I have to think what's next. I'm thinking that I need to go to Chicago and search for some more answers. Find out about the ex-husbands. When I get back, I need to check out Doc Parker's caregiver and have a conversation with Tyler Parker about his father. I will be treading on slippery ice there. Have you had another dream about Doc? Do we have time to investigate?"

"No dreams, but tonight I had an intuitive feeling. Doc is okay for now. I visualized a woman by his side holding his hand. I think it's his caregiver. She's caring for him with great kindness."

"Well, that's good to know, for sure. Look, I'm leaving Friday night for Chicago, late. I have loose ends to tie up at work and I've got to find someone to take Ralph."

"Your son?"

Alex laughs, "Well, he's like my son. He's my dog, man's best friend."

"I'll be happy to take him with me to San Diego on Friday. Bring him tomorrow when you come by, if that's okay? My cat, Maurice, is fine here with my aunt and uncle next door and Magic, my dog, will love another animal companion. My parents have a rescued Golden and will be fine with Ralph coming. We are addicted to dogs. My parents have a lovely yard and there's a dog beach close by."

"Are you sure, Gayle? He's an elderly gentleman I rescued a year ago and he's just that, gentle. He sleeps a lot, and loves other dogs and sleeping on road trips."

"He sounds like a great dog. By the way, please let me reimburse you for your airline fare at least, Alex."

"You're sweet, but I have miles so I'm all set. Look, we found each other to solve this problem for Doc. This is the end of the discussion, okay?"

"Okay," I say reluctantly. "Please, let me take care of Ralph. It's the least I can do."

"Thank you, it's so kind. I'll bring him by your house tomorrow after work so you can meet him."

"Great, I'll cook you my unfamous spaghetti dinner I told you about and the dogs and cat can get to know each other."

"Thank you, Gayle, and one more thing. I know in my heart we are going to keep Doc safe. It's a matter of time but it's come to me that I must delve thoroughly into Evelyn's past to do so."

After we say goodnight, I can hardly sleep in anticipation of helping Doc and thinking about all the info Alex has gathered on Evelyn. I'm still worried about Evelyn pushing Doc in before I get a psychic vibe that she's going to walk him to the pool. Alex sure knows his work. I really don't know anything about him except that his late father was friends with Donnie and a policeman. I wonder what his story is.

Back to Evelyn. I may just have to do a little detective work of my own since I'm not following Evelyn. There's something else, something heaven sent my mind. I close my eyes with stars peeking in the window. I go to sleep under warm covers, hearing the soft breathing of my little twosome in their bed.

I wake up earlier than usual to do sleuth work. After quickly performing my morning routine, I head to Hillsboro before driving to work so I can drive by the back Beach Road behind Doc and Evelyn's house. It's still dark, of course, when I find the spot. There is an overlook below the Parker's neighborhood, and a sign about minimal parking on the small beach access. But a tiny stretch of beach opens up to a nature trail, wrapping up a small hill around the back of the large houses behind her street. It's the perfect place for me to spy on Evelyn and locate where Doc is staying. I drive by the house I think is theirs. I've looked up the addresses on the street and I noted in the internet search that each one has a pool. I find the Parker house for sure, for there is Evelyn's Mercedes parked in front. A silver Lamborghini is parked alongside it. I speed away like a good private eye would. It's Nick's car, I know it is.

Chapter 9
The Best Laid Plans

Prepared with my hair blown out, long jeans, and favorite Mystic Bay cat angel sweatshirt, I open my front door and there stands Alex with Ralph, his German Shepherd. "Welcome! Please come in," I say, as I note how Alex's gentle manner lifts my heart. I compose myself by kneeling down to pet Ralph as Maurice takes a sniff of both man and dog for his approval. He places a paw on Ralph's paw. Ralph looks surprised but not fearful. Alex and I both laugh. "Maurice is king here, as you can tell. Bring Ralph right this way to meet Magic. She will love him."

As we walk through my house to the patio, he remarks, "Of course, I am correct. Your place is so pretty, homey, and great. Wow, your yard is so lush; it's wonderful!"

"Thank you. My aunt and uncle live next door and we help each other out in our gardens with flowers and the vegetable patch."

After the dogs have become used to each other, we sit down for dinner at the antique kitchen table, and I serve him spaghetti with tomato and basil sauce and a little green salad. I pour red wine. We talk of the evidence he's found and the odds of my dream being prophetic. Alex says, "I think we will help Doc with the information from my Chicago trip, the attempted theft, and from your dreams. I'll be home by Friday morning."

We finish and I clear the plates. I bring out the apple torte, warmed in the oven, and this time Alex smiles ear-to-ear.

"Everything was delicious, and now my favorite dessert?" I smile. "Do you want ice cream?"

"Sure, thanks." As I serve the dessert, he talks softly to the dogs, who are still at his feet. Wanting attention too, Maurice meows and jumps to his perch on top of the fridge. "Look at me too," he seems to say. Alex smiles at him: "Funny cat you have there. I love Maurice."

"Yes, he's another animal sent from above. My vet's wife found him in an alley."

"What is wrong with people?" Alex shakes his head, obviously an animal lover like me.

"My friend Maggie says there's a special quality in those who rescue animals."

"She's got that right!"

I serve Alex torte and cut a small piece for me. "It's a recipe from Jack's by The Sea, a restaurant everyone here loves."

He nods. "Yes, I know the place. It's great." I watch him eat, with his kind compliments between bites. I look around my cozy kitchen. I'm happy with my little home. It's all I need in the town I love. I'm staring into space a bit.

"Gayle, I have to tell you what I'm thinking. Please promise me you'll let me handle anything that comes along. I have a feeling you haven't told me something. Am I correct?"

Nervous now, I reply, "Well, yes, yes, this morning before work, I drove by what I believe is Doc and Evelyn's house, and all I can report is that I saw what I believe is Nick's Lamborghini parked by her car. I took a photo of it. Also, I found a road behind their house near the beach. There's a way to view the back of the house if you walk the path up the hill. I feel bad I didn't text you, but I didn't follow her and won't." I worry now what Alex thinks.

"I understand. You have to tell me everything now. Everything you do and think and dream, okay?'"

"Yes, of course."

"This is all very serious, and you need to be in the background now. I'll go with you to scope out the path behind their house, okay?"

"Of course."

"Good. I'll call every day and text from Chicago." He looks down at Ralph and pets the sweet dog, then looks up. "I know Ralph here is in the best of hands."

He smiles but I see something in his eyes, a sadness or worry. He's looking at me but remembering something, I'm guessing. Maybe he thinks I have been foolish snooping around Evelyn and Doc's home and her life.

"What's the matter?" He has seen my own face change. I try to brighten up.

"It's sad to think Evelyn is planning a crime."

"It is and it's very real, Gayle. I know it is. Don't worry, we will help Doc, the two of us." Alex smiles again and I relax. The evening ends and we say goodnight. I watch him wave as he and Ralph get into Buttercup, his Mustang. He's such a good man. Our plan is that I'll pick Ralph up after work and head to San Diego. Mom will advise me about all this. Knowing I have some time yet before anything happens to Doc is good and bad. How much time, I'm not sure. It makes me shiver.

Friday morning is bright and clear; no fog today.

"Well good morning. As you can tell, we're outside our studio on the 44th Street side road. Will you looky here everyone? Wes, our manager, not only approved denim Fridays, but approved my little rescue dog, Magic, here to help me do the weather today. The fog is clearing but we can't see Alcatraz!"

Chapter 10
Home To San Diego

My mother is waiting with opens arms. She and I look alike but her hair is a beautiful, streaked gray with whisps of silver. Her smile is wide and kind. I let the dogs out and we hug and go into the yard. They are two blocks from the sea and the salty air smells like home again in beautiful San Diego,

"This is Magic, Mom and my friend's dog, Ralph, I told you about. Thanks for letting me bring them."

"Of course, dear." Monty, my parents' dog, runs up and all the animals begin to play. Ralph joins right in. Dad emerges from the house with his arms out and his grin wider than Mom's. "Gayle, honey. Wow, you look good, and brought us dogs too?" His laugh is infectious and I'm so glad to be with them. I smell dinner cooking now and feel like I'm finally relaxing, but I have a story for them about what's been going on. It's a story I have to tell them, but I'll wait until our lasagna dinner is done. I'll wait 'til glasses of wine and full stomachs will make the thought of me saving a man's life digestible. I hope.

After dinner, it's blowing hard outside, so Dad sits in his overstuffed favorite chair with his feet propped on the footstool. Mom and I are on the couch drinking decaf and talking. All the dogs sleep on the floor. So, I begin the story, hoping they will understand.

"I have to tell you something, and I know it will be upsetting, but listen, okay?"

"Okay," Dad says with a furrowed brow.

"I dream of an angel sometimes, but a few weeks ago the angel showed me an old, fragile man in danger in the future. Someone will try to push him in a pool. I know who the old man is now because I saw his photo at the fundraiser for Tory's work. He once headed Somerset House for the homeless population. I think his wife is going to push him in the pool sometime soon. It's in the planning stage."

"Oh my," Mom says. "Gayle, you're getting messages like I get. What are you going to do about it? Are you going to the police?"

"I talked to that old college friend I dated briefly, Detective Beau Bolton. He blew me off, but the former Chief of Police of Mystic Bay, Donnie Whitefeather, Uncle Dick's friend, put me in touch with a man named Alex Knight. He's an attorney but has intuition like you do, Mom. He's solved cases for the San Francisco Police. He said his late father was in the department and had the gift of intuition also. He helped solve many cases. I met with Alex, and we have a plan.

"Donnie will be involved, and we will be going to the police soon, but first Alex is investigating the gold digger, second wife Evelyn Parker."

"Is this Doctor Jeremiah Parker, the cardiologist?"

"Yes, Mom. Do you know him?" Mom stands up and goes to the sliding glass doors, the wheels of her mind turning. She's silent but Dad pipes in: "Gayle, when you were young, your mom and I took you and Julian to a birthday party for Dr. Parker's son, Tyler. Julian and Tyler were in camp together, but we'd never met Dr. Parker before, or his nice wife, Harriet. It was at their home in San Francisco. What happened to Harriet?"

"She died," my mom and I say in unison.

"Gayle, you're using your intuition like mine. It's escalating." My mother is tearing up.

"I know, Mom. Evelyn is the younger woman he married who I think is planning to harm her husband, the good doctor."

Dad says, "I remember now, don't you Marie?

Mom says, "I do."

"Remember what?"

Dad continues, "I was holding you in my arms at the birthday party, and as we were introduced to Dr. Parker and his wife, Dr. Parker said an unusual thing to us: "This is one special little girl you have here. She's going to help me someday, somehow. I just know it."

"What? Are you kidding?"

"No, Gayle, your dad and I haven't discussed this for many years. It was quite surprising. It was months before I helped with the April Sorenson case. Then we moved from Mystic Bay to get away from the San Francisco area and the news coverage. I told your dad that Dr. Parker is indeed a psychic. He was calling you in the dream, Gayle. But your angel was helping too. It was meant to be. It's really extraordinary. You have to do this work. You have a team now to help. I will go into my mind and see what I see. But wait. Did you say Alex Knight? His late father must be Tobias Knight, the detective on the April Sorenson case. He knew she was alive and that we would find her far away. When I saw where she was and tracked it on a map, the others were skeptical, but not Tobias. He urged the other policeman to go right away. We drove in the car together. When we found April alive and well, we were thrilled. The man who took her there was scared off by the big bear, little April said. But Tobias and I always knew that the bear who kept her warm and brought her berries to eat was really a Sasquatch." She's quiet a moment, then adds: "Gayle, I am so sorry to hear Tobias has passed away. We kept in touch for a while."

I sit down and really try to take this all in. "This is not a coincidence, Mom. Meant to be for sure. I have to tell Alex all this when he calls."

"Yes, dear," Dad says. "We think Dr. Parker is communicating to you even though he is in a fragile state, and Alex Knight has been sent to you from above."

We talk awhile more, then we go out to say goodnight to the moon and stars in the windy night. The dogs trail behind us. As I go to my childhood bedroom for sleep with dogs in tow, I wonder why Alex didn't check in tonight. It's midnight in Chicago now. I get into my pj's and turn down the covers of my bed, in what is now the guest room in the house. The dogs lay down in dog beds I brought. I text Alex: "I hope you arrived safely. All is well. Call me tomorrow. G."

I immediately get a call from him. "I'm sorry," he says, "I got here an hour ago. I 've been on the phone with a friend with the Chicago Police who will help me with information on Nick and Evelyn's lives in the Chicago area. But something's happened there. What is it?" Alex is blown away by the news. "Yes, my father often spoke of your mother, Marie Russo. This is incredible! We were supposed to meet and work on this case together, just like our parents did. Doc is involved in his own case. This is almost unbelievable, Gayle! Doc's contacting you with his intuitive mind still intact."

Chapter 11
The News From Chicago

Mom and I walked Dog Beach with Magic and Monty. Dad stayed with Ralph bonding, sleeping on the patio in the warmth of the sun like two buddies. Mom had some thoughts last night. I didn't sleep well and tried too hard to communicate with Doc. It didn't work. But my mother said, "It's okay. Now you need to write down things you're thinking of, even if it seems trite. The thoughts you have about Evelyn, the caregiver you said you saw holding his hand, and the most important thought: believe you will solve this and help Dr. Parker. Believe it with all your heart and it will come true. I guessed you have a wonderful connection with Alex."

"Well, he's a great guy; kind and very intuitive. But there's something in his eyes, a twinkle ...yet, Mom, also a worry."

"You will find out soon what it is. There is work for you to do together, but this worry you see will be revealed to you. You need to let this all flow and resolve in your mind. Work together, concentrating on the doctor. Visualize ailing Dr. Parker getting better.

Alex calls as I'm ready for bed again. We talk of how Ralph and Magic are getting along and then he tells me, "I'm having coffee tomorrow with Evelyn's first father-in-law, Baxter Mellon. I've told him who I am upfront, and that I'm working with the San Francisco Police investigating a problem she's involved with."

"Really? I thought we were waiting to notify the police."

"We can't, Gayle. My police detective friend here said we must alert them to your vision in the dream and Evelyn's involvement with Nick Carmeletti. I have spoken to the Chief of Police, and he assigned Beau Bolton to work with us."

Taken aback, I don't say anything about Beau. "I hope this doesn't get out by an informant, like you and I discussed."

"Me too, but we are now involved with Donnie, Beau, and the department, and we will meet with them when we return." He pauses for a moment. "I didn't call Evelyn's first husband, Baxter Mellon Jr. His father informed me on the phone that his son will not discuss Evelyn. After the divorce, he never spoke of her again. He's married now, with a family."

"It's amazing to me that you will be able to talk to her ex-father-in-law."

"Yes, I'll call you tomorrow night and let you know what he says. Have you had any more dreams?"

"No, but I've been asking the angels to help me, and somehow I have a slight memory of when my parents, brother, and I met Doc and Harriet Parker when I was three!"

"This is so unreal. We need to tell Tyler Parker all of this."

"Doc's been calling out to me to help him! Even in his fragile state. I'm leaving to go back to Mystic Bay sooner than expected. Something tells me I need to get home even earlier than I planned, so I will leave day after tomorrow. Please call me tomorrow night."

"Okay, Gayle. This is getting more mysterious as we dig deeper. I'll be home early too, if I can get enough info." Alex laughs and adds, "Oh, and thank you. I appreciate you taking Ralph on a beach vacation."

"He's a love. He fits right in with my parents and Monty. He's Dad's buddy and it's beautiful here in San Diego. I do miss the warmer summers."

"I'd love to see it. Let's go there together when this whole thing is settled for Doc. I'd love to meet your parents."

I am surprised he said this. "Yes, what a good plan. One more thing -- I forgot to tell you, my mother says we should think positive thoughts and prayers for Doc. We must visualize him getting well."

"Your mom is so right."

"Well, goodnight, Alex. I am anxious to hear what you find out. Maybe I'll dream of Doc. I'll also ask the angels to help and send me a message."

"You can do it, Gayle. Sleep well."

"You, too."

We end our call and I snuggle in the covers with dogs below, wondering if Alex really meant it when he said he'd like to meet my parents. He's an amazing man, but then I think of the ring on his finger. It's significant. About to close my eyes. I pray, looking at the stars shine, peeking through my bedroom window. A soft breeze comes through, and I take in a deep breath. "Goodnight, Ralph and Magic," but they are already in sleepyland. Silently, I thank my angel, for doing God's work and bringing Alex Knight my way.

Chapter 12
Evelyn's Fury

After seven hours of driving, thinking about everything, I'm exhausted. Alex called last night and said Nick's been married twice, briefly, to former beauty queens. No kids but many girlfriends over the years. One of the girlfriends was Mrs. Pomeroy, the woman Evelyn tried to steal from. She married a rich doctor and Alex and I concur that Nick sent her to steal the diamonds, possibly diamonds he gave her. It's overwhelming really to think of how things are coming together. The dogs are asleep and I'm so glad to be home as I pull into the carport. "You guys, stay." I get out to unlock my side door. Of course, Maurice runs out of the cat door to welcome us. "Yay, we're home, Maurice! Hope you're okay."

Out of the bushes comes a figure. Oh my God, it's Evelyn Parker! I have no time to think as the dogs start barking. By the porch light, I can see she is angry. Fear runs through my body.

She hisses: "You think you are so smart, Gayle Force, but you are done! Your little friend, Tory, was listening in on my phone call today, so I fired her. But she told me you are telling people I'm neglecting my husband. I am certainly not neglecting my husband! How dare you! I will get YOU fired too. I know the owner of KHBW very well."

I'm about to tell her to get out of my carport but Maurice runs up and bites her ankle. Evelyn tries to kick him off. I shout, "I'm calling the police!" I start to dial 911 but she slaps the phone out of my hand. Just then I hear Uncle Dick's voice shouting as he starts running over to my house. "Gayle, who's there? Who are you? Get away from her!" Evelyn scurries away to her awaiting Mercedes as he approaches. We see her get in her car. We see her speed away.

"Are you alright? That woman, who is she?"

"I know who she is, but we've never met until now. You saved us, Uncle Dick, we are okay, thanks to you!" I explain to Uncle Dick, "It's a misunderstanding between my friend Tory and this woman, her boss." I can't tell him the truth. Giving him a hug, I thank him, and he reluctantly goes back to his house as I walk into mine. Nancy put the lights on for me before I came home. I lock the door and take the dogs and Maurice out to the patio. My homecoming is shattered. What do I do now? Call Alex? I have to.

Our phone conversation is brief, but I feel better. He tells me, "Gayle, this proves you have to stay out of this now. I'll be home tomorrow night. Please call Tory and ask her about this. Tell her not to say anything else and play like you know nothing. I wish I was there. Text me before you go to sleep and lock the doors. But she won't come back, I'm sure."

"I know, I will call Tory. But Alex, you should have seen it. Maurice bit her ankle and Uncle Dick who isn't a runner anymore and has hearing aids, came practically flying over!"

"Angels on earth, Gayle. They're all around us." I feel exhausted. I want this all to go away.

"Please call Donnie tomorrow morning and explain what happened with Evelyn. I will alert Chief Warren and Beau. Listen, you are doing everything right. But I have to tell you that Baxter Mellon explained to me in my interview with him that years ago Evelyn stole money from his home office. She took thousands of dollars he had in a safe. Someone must have helped her, he assumed, someone professional, and we know who that must have been. Nick! His son, Baxter Jr., was furious with his father but did divorce her after his father pressured him, threatening to tell his mother the truth about Evelyn, and that worried him because his mother was ill. I'm hoping to speak to her second husband tomorrow. She's a grifter, a thief, Gayle. It sounds like she steals because she's obsessed with Nick. I think he tells her what to do."

"Me too."

"Text me and keep your phone by your bed. Try not to worry. I'll be there tomorrow. The police will help us, and by the way, you have Maurice the protector."

I laugh for the first time. "Maurice is exhausted but now he's my superhero, like you are."

Oops I shouldn't have said that, but Alex thinks it's funny and says, "I'm trying."

Tory calls on my phone as I'm saying goodbye to Alex, and I take her call.

Tory sounds frightened. She's crying uncontrollably and I have to tell her to stop that. I assure her I'm still her friend and that I'm upset too.

She calms down so I say, "Tory, tell me why you told Evelyn I asked you about Doc's health?"

"I was listening outside her office door," Tory tells me. She was on the phone with a guy and said, 'I love you too, Nick.' She got up quickly and caught me listening. Fired me on the spot. I got so mad and yelled at her. I told her people are wondering if she has a boyfriend and think it's horrible. She asked what people, and I blurted out your name. It was wrong and I am so, so sorry, Gayle."

"Tory, she came out of the shadows when I got home. Scared the living daylights out of me and said she's going to get me fired. She slapped my phone out of my hand! Uncle Dick heard it all and ran over and she sped away in her car. Please, if you encounter her again, leave me out of this. I'll call you soon." I hang up quickly, not really mad at Tory, just mad at myself for asking her about Doc. Could this get any worse now? Do we still have a chance to help Doc now?

I snuggle with the dogs on the couch before I say goodnight and take them to their beds. I text Alex that all is well and Maurice is on guard. This makes me laugh and calm a bit. I put Maurice next to me on my bed. "You're on guard, Super Cat." I close my eyes, wondering how we really can save Doc, who's calling me, who needs me. "Doc Jeremiah, I am trying to help you, but Alex says wait for a dream. I'm waiting. Stay safe Doc."

Chapter 13
The Call And The Night

It's Thursday. I told the station I'd come in since Breezy Bob was filling in for me, but he has a cold. I tossed and turned most of the night, waking up twice to make sure my doors and windows were locked. No dreams of Doc. I roll out of bed and go out to the patio. The stars are shining as I look up and thank God Alex is coming home tonight. As I get dressed, I witness Ralph snuggling with Magic on the bathroom rug as Maurice sits nearby. They have become the three amigos. I wish Alex could see this. I'm thinking about him all day long now. How he dropped into my life in the synchronicity of it all, how he calms me and builds me up. Alex is my partner in helping Doc. Why does he wear a wedding ring? When he held me that night in the parking lot of The Bayview Club, I felt a feeling I never get with a man, a security, a bond. I shut this out of my mind now. Driving to work, I detour up to Sea Grape Circle and Doc's house for a drive by. The mist is thick, but I can still see. There it is -- Nick's car again. As I drive out, I decide to walk up the path behind the house after work today. My intuition starts to rise; she's going to take Doc to the pool soon. But when? Will it really happen or am I wishing this whole thing was over? I know Alex said he would walk the path with me. I'll text him that I'm going on my own today as time is of the essence.

I arrive at work and my boss, Wes, walks by me and greets me like he knows nothing of Evelyn's warning. "Thanks for coming in, Gayle. Breezy Bob's under the weather today." He laughs and I thank the Lord our owner of the station hasn't heard from Evelyn. But I'm shocked when I have a voicemail.

"Hello, Gayle Force? This is Sandra Garcia. I take care of a man, Dr. Jeremiah Parker. He doesn't say much but we watch your show every morning and he says, 'My Angel' when he sees you on TV. It's really nice because it's God's will, I know.

Can you call me?" She leaves her cell number, and I am flabbergasted but have to report the weather before I can text Alex. I try to act cheerfully and I almost act over the top. Mark, Jeni, and the whole crew laugh when I sing the weather: "I lost my sunshine, in San Francisco!" I put my hands on my hips and declare, "Yes, gloom June ends with a BIG BIG BANG. No sun all day!" Then I sing the line from a Ronno song: "We all need the sunshine and rain!" I think I'm losing it.

My text back from Alex affirms my decision. Calling Sandra Garcia from my cell phone on my break, I am nervous but steady with a smile on my face. She answers with a Spanish accent.

"Bueno, this is Sandra."

"Sandra, hi. This is Gayle Force, meteorologist at KHBW TV. Thank you for your kind voicemail."

"Oh Miss Gayle. Oh, you are so pretty and nice on TV and my Dr. Parker here just loves watching you. He's waking up now. Would you like to talk to him?"

Stunned, I say, "Sure."

There is a pause and then his weakened voice comes on the phone. It's Doc!! I recognize his voice from my dream.

"Hi, Angel."

Then a pause as Sandra puts the phone back to her ear. "Miss Gayle, you heard him. He loves you because you are so sweet on TV. It's funny. Dr. Parker don't talk much all day but once and a while he says, "Harriet", his wife who died a few years ago."

I don't know what to say for a moment, and then the response comes. "Well, you tell him, Sandra, I am here anytime you all want to call, okay? You watch on Friday; my little dog will be making an appearance with me. Please call me anytime. This is my cell phone."

"Oh, we will. I put you in my phone now. Thank you, Miss Gayle."

"No, thank you for liking the show. Maybe we will meet one day in person, okay? Have a sunshiny day and take care of Dr. Parker."

"Oh, of course. You have no idea how hard I try."

After we hang up, I wish I could have said more. I would have told her, "But I do know all and hopefully I will meet you soon and Doc will be away from danger."

I text Alex that I made the call, and he texts back. He thinks that Sandra Garcia's contacting me is a sign from the angels that she will help us save Doc. His message says, "We have her number now and she has yours. I'll call you from the airport."

After work, I take the turn for Hillsboro. I've changed into sweats and a jacket. A cap is on my head as I park near the path. No one is in the four-slot parking area. It's been cloudy all day and even a renegade raindrop is falling now. It's a bit of a climb but there's a path made of sand and small gravel. There's a wood railing and obviously it's a path for residents of Sailor's Cove to take down to the beach from the back of their houses. I time it, and it takes about eight minutes to get to the back of Doc's house. It will take more time at night, I'm sure. The casita where Doc stays is at the rear. Small windows face the path and to the west is a swimming pool. The big house looms in front of it. There are bushes but I note a gate about thirty yards away. There is a streetlight in front, to the side of the big house. That will give us enough light at night, I'm guessing.

It's after eleven now, and I'm prepared. I wish Alex was here, but I convinced him not to come late to pick up Ralph, that he could pick him up tomorrow morning. I told him I'd put the key under the mat.

As I get ready for what I believe will be happening tonight, I think about Alex. As I look in the mirror to put on the wig, I notice my face flush as I think about him. How can this be? I'm in love? The man is kind, considerate, diligent, caring, and smart. He seems to be very focused on my safety and believes one hundred percent of what I believe. His eyes are twinkling blue. I make myself stop thinking about him now. Maurice is in the laundry room, which is behind the carport. It's not attached to the house and sometimes I put him there if people come over who are allergic to cats. He's in his cat carrier with the door shut. Ralph and Magic are safe and asleep at Aunt Nancy and Uncle Dick's. I told them I was coming home late from a party and would pick Magic up after work, but Alex would come in the morning to pick up Ralph. I had to tell them a lie. The only light on is the porch light in front and the night lights in the kitchen and my bathroom. Why didn't I tell Alex what I fear might happen? Because what if I am wrong? What if I said my intuition told me someone was going to break in tonight?

Wearing all black with black make up dotted under my eyes like a football player, I'm ready. I wait for several minutes until I know I hear the intruder. My heart races. I assume it's a male, not Evelyn. That's what my psychic vibe told me, anyway. I hear very light footfalls on the tile. He's about to enter the darkened hall with only the dimmest light coming from the window and streetlight outside. Is it Nick? I stand behind the wall of the guest bathroom. The light from the streetlight only makes out his form. He walks by me and in a flash, it seems I've hit him on the back of his head with the seashell lamp Aunt Nancy made for me. I was good at soft ball but bang him just hard enough, I hope, to knock him out. My adrenaline hits and I turn on the hall light.

"Guiseppi?" He's writhing on the floor, groaning. What will I do now? I grab my phone and dial 911.

Guiseppi tries to get up but can't. All of a sudden, Alex runs in the hall. "Alex!"

"Gayle, are you okay?" Donnie is right behind him, and they run over to Guiseppi and secure his hands with hand cuffs. Donnie searches Guiseppi. "No weapons," he says to Alex. How did they know this was happening? Guiseppi doesn't struggle as he comes to. Aunt Nancy's shell lamp is mostly intact, but the base is broken off. I pick up the lamp and base, holding it all close to me. I find I'm breathing heavily.

Then in a weakened voice, Guiseppi says, "I only wanted to look at her." Guiseppi seems dazed. How did he know where I live? Why is he here? Oh, no. Of course, Nick sent him!

A few minutes later Beau and two other policemen come in the house and lift him up, securing Guiseppi with their big arms to take him away. Beau walks behind them as Mystic Bay Police Chief Jim Cero comes into the hall. There is much confusion and talking. I set the lamp in the bathroom, dazed myself. In a few minutes, Beau comes back in the house, giving me an angry look as I take off the wig. He says to me, "Why didn't you tell us someone might break in?"

I decide to be calm and not speak, but what I want to say is because you, of all people, wouldn't have believed me.

Beau looks at Alex with disgust. "I suppose you knew about this and put Gayle in danger with your psychic bull."

Alex doesn't respond, acting as if Beau didn't say anything. He looks only at me, "Gayle, I knew something was happening. Your phone was on 'do not disturb' every time I texted. I know you keep your cell on at night. You've said so. I rushed to my car, trying to make sense of what could be happening. It came to me as I turned on the highway. I woke up Donnie and Chief Warren, then Jim Cero."

"You could have called me, but oh no, Chief Warren called me!" Beau is still angry, and at other times I would have thought about how cute he looked in his sweats. But as I look at his frowning face, I can't help it. I say, "I couldn't count on you."

He's mystified: "What?" I ignore him as Alex says to me, "I get it. You weren't sure if you were right, I know the feeling." Jim Cero says, "Do you know this man? "Yes," I tell him, "Guiseppi. I don't know his last name, but he works as a server at Nick's Catch in San Francisco. I went in there one night but didn't use a credit card, so how did he know who I was? I was wearing this wig so he couldn't have recognized me from TV.

Beau seems frenzied. "What? Wearing a wig? So you were stalking Evelyn Parker at that restaurant connected to the Mafia? Oh, this is beautiful Gayle, just beautiful."

Alex says with disgust, "Why don't you go and do your duty and book the guy? Or shall we ask Chief Warren for a different detective to help us here?" My eyes widen as Beau, of course, has the last word: "This psychic craziness has gotten you in trouble now, both of you." He huffs, practically stomping behind the policeman. Chief Cero says, "I need a statement."

We all go into the living room. I sit stiffly on the couch, wondering what to say? I put my hands to my face and tears flow. Alex puts his arm around me, and I stop.

"I didn't want to tell anyone because, well, I thought, what if I was wrong." Beau walks back in.

"You weren't wrong, Gayle." Alex's face seems melancholy now.

Donnie says, "It's time to tell Jim all that's going on. Chief Warren and Beau know now, and so we have to plan what to do next. "

Beau, who is still seething, says, "This is insane. You guys, this may not work, you know."

Alex ignores Beau and explains all that's gone on with the dream and the case so far.

Donnie says, "Let's plan on meeting tomorrow at two at The Next Door Café." He looks at Beau. "We all have to be on board."

"I am," says Beau and he leaves, not looking at Alex or me or even saying goodbye. After Donnie and Jim leave, Alex says, "I'm staying the rest of the night Gayle. I'll sleep on the couch, but I don't want you alone. I'll go over and pick up the dogs tomorrow at your aunt and uncle's."

I tell him he can stay in my office, the guest room. Donnie calls, apparently to tell us Guiseppi Grimaldi will be booked in San Francisco County Jail. Aunt Nancy and Uncle Dick never woke up, nor did any neighbors, oddly enough. I take sleepy-eyed Maurice out of the laundry room, show Alex the towels in the bathroom, and say goodnight. "You better not let your halo get rusty," I say with a smile.

"What?" Alex seems almost alarmed.

"I mean, thank you. You were like an angel dropping in from the sky tonight." I smile at him but he still looks stunned at my words.

"Gayle, you are made of magic. Just like your dog, little Magic. You came into my life when I was wondering how I could help the world more and now I know. We are going to help Doc." That's all he says, as he makes sure my doors are locked. I'm not sure what to say, but I tell him, "Seriously, you saved me tonight. I was wrong not to tell you. I have only a few hours before I have to get up. I'll try to be quiet when I leave."

"Your psychic vibe continues to grow. Goodnight now and try to rest."

I have two hours to sleep but I take a shower, washing off the makeup, then fall into bed; secure knowing Alex is in the next room and Maurice is sleeping under the covers with me. I dream of my father, Joe. We are walking on the beach, he in white. His black wavy hair blows in the breeze. He tells me he's sorry he couldn't stay, that I have a beautiful soul. Then the scene changes and my angel is there on the beach. Her brown hair tied in the back like a ponytail. She shows me the scene: Doc is walking to the edge of the pool. Evelyn is behind him. With a start I awake, to the smell of coffee.

"For you," Alex says when I walk into the kitchen at four. I ask him, "Why are you up?"

"I couldn't sleep. I'm going to stay here tonight after the meeting. We can discuss everything we need to do then."

"We won't need a meeting. It's happening tonight. The angel and my father came to me in my dream.

"Oh, wow. I'll get everything ready and contact Donnie, Tyler Parker, and the police. You and I will walk up the path early and signal when Evelyn walks out. That's how I see it happening. Okay?"

"Yes, thank you, Alex, for your belief in my dreams and for your help."

"You're welcome, Gayle," he says as he hands me the coffee with a smile on his face. "Now drink it down. We'll need a lot of caffeine today to save Doc." I'm befuddled one more time at the actions of this kind, wonderful man. I want to hug him goodbye, but don't. He hasn't given me any indication this is possibly becoming anything more than friendship.

Chapter 14

Saving Doc

I report the weather as cheerfully as I can. I go into my office at ten and can't help it. I fall asleep for a few minutes, but my cell phone rings. It's Sandra Garcia.

"Oh, Miss Gayle, I'm so glad I got you. Doc says his Angel is coming for him tonight."

My intuition gives me the words I know I must say: "Dear Sandra, yes. Doc will be safe tonight. Tyler and I will come late. But you mustn't say anything to anyone." Somehow, I know I can trust her and then I know I am right when she responds, "God is good, I won't tell no one you are coming. I have been praying Tyler would come."

"I have your cell number," I say. "I will call you when I can. It will be late." I call Alex, telling him of Sandra's message. He replies, "This is no coincidence, Gayle. Doc knows you are coming for him. He's an intuitive. He knew it somehow years ago when he met you as a child that you'd help him in some way."

As I do my final weather segment, everyone says, "Have a good day!" I wave and hope God and His angels are watching and waiting.

I hurry home to find Magic, Ralph, and Maurice sitting with Aunt Nancy and Uncle Dick on the couch. Alex greets me at the door: "I met your lovely Aunt and Uncle. I said we will tell them what is going on when you came home. I fixed sandwiches and coffee."

Aunt Nancy starts, "Tell us, dear, what is going on? We were surprised when Alex met us here at the door and told us you both were working with the police."

"Yes, Aunt Nancy," I say, sitting down. All the animals run to me, even Ralph. I rub their ears. "I had a dream of an old man in trouble. Through Donnie, I met

Alex, who is an intuitive and has worked with the police like Mom does. Tonight, we will be working with the police's help to save the man from harm."

"Gayle, just like Marie, you have the extraordinary ability!" Uncle Dick is more than surprised.

"Yes, I guess so, Uncle Dick. We will be fine but home very late tonight. Can you keep the dogs and put Maurice in the laundry room for one more night?"

"Of course, dear," says Aunt Nancy.

But Uncle Dick seems suddenly more concerned. "Have you told your mother and dad? They will surely worry."

"I plan on calling today. When we are safe and it's over, I will text you, okay? It'll be late."

They agree. The atmosphere changes as Alex says, "Let's eat these turkey and cheese sandwiches because we all need food for the coming hours." I smile at Alex and feel thankful for him and for the love of my aunt and uncle. The dogs and cat beg for turkey and, of course, they get their way.

......

It's dark as Alex and I walk the path traversing behind the houses on Sea Grape Circle. I lead the way. We are in dark clothing, prepared with flashlights, phones with sound turned off, and backpack with towels and a first aid kit. The wind is chilly and my face feels numb, but my adrenaline is rushing through my veins. We stop in full view of Doc's house. The casita's lights are on, as well as the lights in the pool area. I check my watch. It's exactly 11:30.

Beau, Tyler, Donnie, and their team are parked on the next street over in an unmarked van. They will travel onto Sea Grape in ten minutes at scattered intervals. Beau will yell out Evelyn's name at the front gate that leads to the back yard, hopefully before she pushes Doc in the pool or before we can get him to safety. We will text "yes" to Beau when Evelyn appears with Doc. As the minutes tick by the waiting seems endless. I find I'm sweating in the cold and shivering at the same time. Alex puts his hand on mine. He whispers, "We're ready." Just as he says it, Doc appears out of his doorway with a walker and Evelyn all in black behind him. "Harriet, Angel," Doc calls.

"No, Jeremiah!" Her voice sounds frightened. But Doc speaks again. "Angel."

Alex presses "yes" and sends the text. Evelyn walks with Doc with her hand on his arm. As they near the edge, I move and brush a large branch. Evelyn turns to look my way. She then hesitates. Beau is at the front gate and busts it open, shouting, "Evelyn Parker, halt!" Evelyn seemingly tries to hold on Doc's arm, but Doc begins to fall. Alex is there, moving so fast in front of Doc that there is no way he will fall anywhere but in Alex's arms. Evelyn starts crying and Beau and team rush in and handcuff her arms behind her back. Evelyn screams, "What are you doing?" I'm frozen like a statue for a moment. We've saved Doc! Tyler rushes in and takes his father in his arms. Dr. Burns comes and they take Doc away by ambulance to the local hospital as the police remove Evelyn.

Chapter 15
Doc And His Angels

We get home before 1 a.m. I texted Sandra Garcia and Aunt Nancy, letting them know that Doc's safe and at St. Mary's Hospital. My house has the light on in the kitchen. First, I take Maurice out of the laundry room. The dogs are next door, safe and sound. Alex and I both look at each other, exhausted. Alex says with a smile, "We did a heavenly deed tonight. It all went without a hitch. Doc is in the hospital with Tyler by his side."

I smile back: "Yes, it's a miracle. We know Nick knows now and is most likely already stacking lawyers behind her. But we'd better get to bed. It's so late, and I have to be up in two hours."

"Goodnight, Gayle, Doc's angel."

"Goodnight, Doc's other angel." I laugh and then, in a small act of affection, he smiles, kissing me on the cheek. Startled, I kiss him back on his cheek. I feel a flutter and wish he would kiss me on the lips, but he doesn't. It's okay, I have started to have feelings for him, but I won't make the first move. Alex smiles, even though there is still a look of worry in his eyes. "Now, goodnight and see you at four."

"You don't have to get up with me again, Alex. You need to rest." I am sure I'm blushing but he says, "No, you need your coffee maker, me." He kisses me on the forehead, walks to the side door making sure it's locked, and goes to the other bathroom. I head to my room. I take a shower, letting the lavender suds fall around me. Tonight, we helped save Doc, and Alex, the most extraordinary man in the world, kissed me on the cheek and forehead! There is something about him that shines, I think, as I get into bed. The stars are out and also shining at me from my window. I feel safe knowing Alex is here and a few hours' sleep without worrying about Doc sounds like a dream come true.

Chapter 16

The News

When I get to the newsroom, it's all abuzz with the news of Dr. Jeremiah Parker, but the police have kept Alex's and my name out of the reports. Chief Warren demanded it as the investigation is on-going. As Mark, our anchor, reports the story, I listen as an innocent viewer would. He states: "An unknown couple was there at the right time as the renowned cardiologist, Dr. Jeremiah Parker, was led by his wife to his pool at midnight. His wife, Evelyn Parker, is accused of trying to cause bodily harm to her husband but the police and the unknown couple stopped her from pushing him in the pool. The police say that Evelyn Parker was booked into San Francisco County Jail last night. Prudence Coca has the story. Prudence."

"Yes, we are outside the jail speaking to Mrs. Evelyn Parker's attorney, Victor Vayne, standing with Mrs. Parker, who has been released on one million dollars bail. Mr. Vayne, do you have any comment for us this morning?"

"Yes, young lady," Vayne retorts. "The evidence will prove that two so-called psychic detectives planned this whole event to frame poor Mrs. Parker." Evelyn wipes her eyes. She doesn't say anything but looks a little worse for wear in a gray suit with a white button-down collar and blue scarf. Her hair is slicked back in a little mussed bun, and she has no make-up on but the reddest of lipsticks. She wants to talk but her lawyer puts his hand up to prevent her from speaking and they whisk away in awaiting black Cadillac SUV.

I tell the weather with a little skip of lightheartedness: "Good Thursday everyone, one beautiful morning. It's Weather Dog Day! My dog Magic is here now, saying hello to you all. Today, nothing but blue skies after the Bay Area mist clears, but great sailing weather with a soft sea breeze. Right now, it's a perfect time for your second cup of coffee or tea before work."

How on earth did Alex get to Doc before he fell in the pool? it happened so fast and I just stood there. We will not be named until a trial is set. But a fearful feeling comes over me. Will someone leak our names? Would it be Nick, the sneak, or the criminal, Carmeletti?

Chapter 17

The Blind Date

Well, it's a been a week since we got Doc away from Evelyn. He's at Tyler's house in Pacificside, the town next to Hollyvale, where Alex grew up. Doc's there recuperating with Sandra Garcia and her husband by his side as caregivers. Tyler says Doc's making great progress with PT, OT, and speech therapy. Dr. Burns is cooperating and has talked to the police and prosecutor. We know he tried his best and it will all be revealed at the trial.

I've seen Alex once at the police station, where of course, unfortunately, Beau, interviewed us along with the prosecuting attorney, the brilliant and beautiful Katerina Lopez. It was awkward but Alex and I were honest and acted professional. As I was leaving, Beau took me aside and said, "I'd like to take you on a date again. Unless you've hooked up with Alex." Beau seems so pathetic to me, but not wanting to be unkind I said, "I'm sorry, Beau, it just wouldn't work. Thank you, though." I turn and walk to Alex, who's waiting.

Alex and I have lunch at The Half Time Grill. We discuss the case and I'm picking up the vibe Alex is thinking of me only as his partner in helping Doc. So be it. The twinkle is in his baby blue eyes when he looks at me, but the worry or whatever it is, sadness maybe, is still there. We talk candidly about what happened and the fact that our names will be out in the media soon. I explain I will let my boss know my involvement in the Evelyn Parker case tomorrow. I don't know how that will fare.

"I have a good feeling about it, Gayle," Alex tells me. "You're very popular with the audience. You're made of magic, remember? As magic as your little dog landing on your doorstep the night you realized it was Doc you were dreaming about."

With a twinkle of my own, I reply, "And your halo still is not getting rusty." He looks at me with that look of worry again, but still smiles.

As we say goodbye, I realize how much I miss talking to Alex daily, but I have to move forward. A kiss on the forehead and cheek are not indicative of falling in love, and so I accepted Maggie's offer. Tonight, at 7 pm, I will walk into Jack's by The Sea and meet my mystery date. Maggie insists it will be rejuvenating for me to meet him. I didn't tell her much about Alex. She knows he's nice, kind, and handsome too. She's just glad we helped Doc and can move forward now. Anyway, I arrive at my house and have a happy homecoming greeting by Maurice and Magic. It's as if they haven't seen me in a year. I feed them and then shower with my lavender suds and put on my favorite denim pantsuit again. I want to have a different memory wearing it than my meeting with Beau at Pal's Captain Inn. I blow my hair out long and put on the giant gold hoop earrings Mom and Dad gave me for Christmas last year. Mom calls and we talk about the date tonight. "Enjoy," she said. "But remember, I do feel that Alex is going to ask you out at some point."

"Yes, Mom. I wish he was my date tonight. I'm okay. Don't worry." After we hang up, I decide to drive the short distance. Once there, I quickly get out of my car, realizing I'm a tad bit late, but that's okay. I hurry into the restaurant and say to the hostess, "Hi, I'm meeting the Greenstreet party."

"Right this way ma'am," The smells from the kitchen make me even more hungry, a mixture of surf and turf. I hope this guy is nice. I see Maggie waving from a table by the ceiling to floor window. The sea behind her is gorgeous with the sun setting an orange glow into the foamy waves. It's halfway blinding but I see Noah is talking to a man. My blind date turns to me. What? it's Alex! I stand there for a moment taking it all in. He looks so handsome. Walking up to them, all of them stand. I hug Maggie then Noah then I turn to Alex.

"Well, fancy meeting you here!" Alex laughs, and so do Maggie and Noah.

Standing like a statue for one more moment, as they all continue laughing, I finally ask, "Was this all planned a while ago?" I put my hands on my hips pretending to be mad, but of course they know it's all in jest.

Alex confesses, "I knew about it, yes, from the start, but Maggie didn't know. However, she guessed early on. Noah and I went to college together."

"Yes," says Maggie. "When Noah said Alex's name, I figured out an attorney Alex who lived in San Francisco had to be the man Gayle said was her partner."

Of course, I feel comfortable around Alex, and it feels really natural to be with my best friend, her husband, and the man I have strong feelings for. They order shrimp cocktail and swordfish, but I stick with the salad, clam chowder, and sourdough bread. We order wine and quietly speak of the case but then we turn to personal matters.

Maggie says, "Alex, you grew up in Hollyvale. What a lovely town."

"It is. It's not far from beaches, quiet and friendly. By the way, my late father, Tobias, was an intuitive also. He was on the San Francisco Police Force before we moved to Hollyvale and worked closely with Gayle's mom on the April Sorenson case. He told me what an amazing psychic she was. She drew the exact location on a map, twenty-five miles from the abduction spot, where April would be found."

Maggie and Noah find this not a coincidence, and of course, I agree. There are no coincidences.

The talk changes to how Maggie and I met at camp in the summers and how Alex and Noah met in college days. Noah says, "We were in the same dorm and started thinking thoughts at the same time. We both knew we were intuitive. I stayed to get my Master's in creative writing and Alex went to law school in Arizona. Now, here we are. You two might have met at our wedding but there were so many people at the reception here at Jack's by The Sea. I think I am correct -- you both had dates?" Alex and I look at each other and agree. He gazes at me with those twinkling eyes that still hold a worry or a secret. We both tell them what a beautiful reception it was and that the food, just as tonight's food, was fabulous. Unfortunately, we finish eating and the surprise double date ends.

We leave the restaurant with hugs and laughter. We wave goodbye to Maggie and Noah. Alex says, "I'll see you tomorrow, after you get off work at the station. We'll go see Doc, then we'll head over to the restaurant I told you about. I want to take you to a place in Hollyvale where my family used to go for hot dogs."

"Great! But I know what you are going to ask next. I do eat the occasional hotdog, Alex," I laugh. "Plenty of onions and mustard for me." We have a quick hug. No big kiss, and I know in my heart something is stopping him. What could it be? Another woman possibly?

When I get home, I take Magic out for a stroll around the block. Then I go out by myself, walking the short distance to the beach. It's 9:30, the stars are out, and the streetlights shine on the calming sea. There are couples walking along holding hands, and I so wish I could be with Alex, but he didn't ask to come over. I pick up a lone shell and throw it back in the waves. They capture it in their gentle foam. I think of Alex one more time. I ask the angels out loud, "What to do, dear angels?" This time, a thought runs through my head: "Be patient." But I wonder, is a hot dog lunch a date?

I know now, there are no coincidences. Only serendipity and synchronicity. I was meant to meet Alex. Revolving doors of boyfriends and the degrading relationship with Beau make me realize that Alex is the type of man to fall in love with. But if not him, then maybe someone else will come along.

Later, I lay quietly in my bed surrounded by my happy home. I'm nurtured by my animals' love and thoughts of family that are so dear. "Goodnight my angels on earth and angels above. Doc, God bless you. See you tomorrow." But there is a nagging thought, and a momentary sentence crosses my brain from the angels. This surprises me: "Evelyn needs your prayers."

Chapter 18
Doc And A Shell

I'm waiting in Tyler and Pam's driveway. Alex drives up in Buttercup; it's good to see him, but I'm on guard a little now.

Tyler greets us warmly with thank yous and hugs. We walk to the sunporch where Doc sits in a recliner with Sandra Garcia and a man I'm sure is her husband. The sixtyish Sandra is beautiful, with a head of thick, black hair tied in a long ponytail. We hug and she introduces us to Eduardo, her husband, who apparently doesn't speak much English. Alex greets them and we both sit down next to Doc. He takes one of each of our hands. "Thank you." He turns to me. "Angel." Tyler explains Doc's situation. A stroke left him weak, but in two short weeks with us, he's made many strides. We don't say anything to anyone in the room about the case. We have been told not to. We only know our part in the investigation. So, when we say goodbye to Doc, Sandra holds me close and says, "I will call you one day; you and I will have lunch at my favorite Mexican Cantina afterwards, okay?"

Tyler walks us out. "I've taken over Dad's Somerset House as acting CEO," he tells us. "Evelyn is still in the house, but I will help Dad file papers to divorce her as he becomes more aware of everything. It may take until after the trial. Dad will not be at the trial, but I will. I can never stop thanking you both. You saved my father's life. God bless you." We leave with hugs and well wishes. I follow Alex in my car to the beach restaurant named Sugar Shack. It's not really a restaurant -- rather a hotdog stand. But it's cute and in walking distance to the beautiful stretch of beach.

I look at the familiar stretch of sand and pewter sea because I had a dream last night. I dreamed of Alex's parents. Their faces were not clear to me as they strolled on the beach. Tobias, his father, handed Rachel, his mother, a shell that was entwined in a circle. The sea birds swirled around them. Tobias said something and placed the shell on Rachel's finger. It is then I woke up.

I look above at the bright, sunny but chilly July day. Alex walks up and announces, "Let's eat!" We walk in the cute Sugar Shack, adorned with seashore rope and fake shell decorations and wrought iron tables and chairs. He orders at the counter. "Best hotdogs in the US, and curly fries too."

As we start to eat, I decide to bring up the dream of his parents.

"I had a dream last night, and in it your parents were walking along this very beach. I couldn't see their faces, but your dad handed your mom a shell formed into a ring and placed it on her finger."

"Amazing Gayle. Yes, that's how they met, exactly as they told me, but there's more. This is where they were married weeks later." He has that look still in his eyes, so I say, "I'm sure you miss them terribly."

"Yes, but I know they are together for sure." He pauses, then adds, "Uh, I need to tell you something, but I want to hold off 'til after the trial, if you can possibly wait."

An alarm bell goes off in my mind, but I stay calm. "What is it? You have worry in your eyes."

"I want to see you, but I just need to think about some things I would have to explain to you about my life. I have my reasons."

My heart drops and I don't know what to say. My head lowers, my eyes moisten.

Alex continues, "I care about you more than you realize. Until the trial is over, I want to have dinners out and at your house and stroll on the beach and get to know each other better. Then perhaps I'll be ready to tell you so many things about my life. I loved our date last night."

I can't speak and he continues, "Can you possibly understand?"

"I can, sort of, Alex. You have your reasons, but I have made a decision. I won't be able to get together for a while. My boss wants me to go on leave from the station starting Monday until after the trial. I'm taking the animals with me to my parents' house for a few weeks to get away from it all. I know the news media will have a blast with our names coming out in the news tomorrow." Alex seems surprised.

My hot dog is getting cold but I can't pick it up.

"Really? Okay, of course, I understand."

"Look, you've been an amazing detective partner and we will be in touch about the trial, okay? I'm sorry, I need to go." I get up and he seems stunned. "Wait, please!"

I turn around. He says, "I will call you every night, okay? We have to stay in touch. Maybe I could come down to San Diego in a few weeks. Maybe by then I'll be able to tell you everything about me."

"Okay. Well, goodbye for now." I am out the door in thirty seconds. Hurrying to my car, tears are streaming, but I'm okay. I'm okay. Angels, be with me.

Chapter 19
The Stillness And The Sea

We walk on the beach every morning and night. Mom and I talk. My mother insists Alex is in love with me and I with him and that it will all work out. "If he has something to mull over before he tells you, let him. He must need this time, this space."

Dad feels that some men get scared when a woman is so beautiful. Dad tells me later, "I was scared to ask your mother out all those years ago. She was too beautiful for me, I thought. But then I realized real beauty comes from within and her soul was meant for me. I knew we were to be together, and my insecurities fled."

Very kind words from my parents. But now, at their home, I try to think positively about my life without Alex. I enjoy the stillness at night. I curl up with a book with my animals in my old room. Many days, I go with Mom to the Food Kitchen and pack groceries for families in need. I help with dinner and smile and laugh with my wonderful family, but I can't escape my thoughts of Alex. How can I? He calls every night like clockwork. We talk about the case. There are a lot of things we don't know. Sandra is a big witness and so is Baxter Mellon, with his story of Evelyn and the money stolen out of the safe. But we are not privy to the whole investigation. Dixie Pomeroy, whose jewelry was stolen by Evelyn, is a witness also. Plus, there is a mystery witness. We can't imagine who could that be. Last night, at the end of the conversation, he said, "I'm sorry if I hurt you. I'll explain soon."

Tonight, it's been three weeks since I left Mystic Bay, but he calls. "I'm coming this Friday to spend a few days. But would it be okay with your mom and dad?"

"Of course." My heart lifts and I tell him I had already let them know he might come visit. As Friday arrives, I fix my hair a thousand times but decide on the usual ponytail. Then he appears, with yellow roses. I ask him, "How did you know they are my favorite?"

"I asked Noah to ask Maggie," he replies. He also brought red roses for my mother. How did he know those were her favorites? Mom and Dad love him from "hello" at the front door. He tours the house accompanied by Ralph, who was invited too. So as the dog and cat clan are reunited and Monty is part of it all, we sit down to Margaritas. The smell of the ocean nearby and the beautiful breeze and sunset nurture our spirits. Of course, I eat heartily of the vegetable lasagna, salad, and dessert of brownies. We talk of the trial, but also of my mom working with Alex's father so long ago, and how it's come full circle with the two of us. Mom and Dad say goodnight early and Alex and I are alone in the great room by the gas fireplace, dogs at our feet. Monty has gone to bed with my parents and Maurice has dibs on my lap.

Alex finally speaks: "It's time to tell you my truth."

I feel nervous and not able to say anything.

"When you told me that day not to let my halo get rusty, I thought maybe you knew."

"What, you are an angel?" I've almost shouted and laughed loudly but put my hand over my mouth. My eyes are wide open and so is my mouth.

Alex takes my hand, "No, I'm not an angel. This is a secret you must keep, please, or I can't tell you. A secret for life?"

"Yes, I can keep secrets, Alex. I promise."

"My mother met my father walking down the beach. She was sent to meet him, and she wanted to live an earth experience for a while. Heaven sent her to meet a shy man with extraordinary abilities: my father."

"Heaven sent your mom?"

"Yes, Gayle. My mother, Rachel, is truly an angel sent from above. She came to earth to be with him, love him, and have a child. Dad was over the moon with happiness. They had me and we all had the most precious life together in

Hollyvale. One year ago, when Dad was ill, my mother told me she had to go with him when he passed away. She insisted, though, that if I didn't want her to go, she would stay. I couldn't tell her to please stay for me, because their love was a love like no other. I'm a grown man now but really, Gayle, I am half angel with the psychic ability from my father's side. Angels are not psychic."

He continues: "Mom took me flying when I was a child. I'd hold my dog, Tuffy, and we would fly over the gleaming ocean when the moon was full. We flew over the farms at night when the air was fresh from the scent of the crops. The animals, dogs and cats on the farms and in town, would look up at us, knowing an angel and her little boy were flying above. How I wish I could take you flying, but I can't fly. Yet there are angels living as humans. They are here to guide and help the townsfolk. But it is a secret to keep forever."

I look at Alex who is telling me the truth. I never have thought of angels living as humans sent to help us. I know angels are real and have had experiences with them, but Alex, a half angel?

"Who are angels? Are there half angels like you? Do you know any?"

"I only knew my mother, but she said there were many. She was so intent on keeping the secret. She said when you find the right woman, she will be the one you marry but you must be careful. The secret will still be the biggest secret in the world. So, since I found the one I want to marry, I can't keep this in any longer. Will you marry me before the trial, after the trial, whenever?"

I close my eyes and listen to the stillness of the night. I open them and see his worried hurt expression has turned soft and calm. "Yes, of course. I'll marry you, my half angel." We fall into each other's arms and our kiss seems never-ending. We decide to talk more in the morning. I insist Alex stays with me in my room tonight as the dogs and cat trail behind, not wanting to miss out on a group family sleep. As we get into bed it seems so natural to be with him. "I'm going to wake up with a half angel," I say as we turn out the light.

"I'm the one waking up with an angel," he says. "Thank you. I love you Gayle Force, soon to be my wife." As the breeze blows softly through the window curtains and the sounds of the dogs and cat breathing lulls us like a lullaby in the stillness, we fall asleep, and wake wrapped in each other's arms. We will tell my parents the news of our love and marriage, but the secret will be safe forever.

Chapter 20
The Wedding

As we come home, we start planning our wedding. Where do we decide to go to plan it? The Sugar Shack, of course. It almost makes me forget about the possibility of returning to my job. The paper was full of headlines: "KHBW's Meteorologist, Gayle Force, is psychic witness in trial of the year! Did the wealthy CEO, Evelyn Parker, attempt to kill her husband, Dr. Jeremiah Parker?" But I can't think of that now. My family and friends are thrilled for us. The trial will just be a part of our lives. We helped save Doc and that's all that matters.

I asked Alex how he got to Doc so fast that fateful night so Doc didn't fall in the pool, and his explanation is extraordinary.

"Evelyn seemed to hesitate, and I was a runner and sprinter in school. I had to hold myself back because I could run faster than anyone. That's how I was able to get to Doc so fast. Sometimes my feet would seem to lift off the pavement as they did getting to Doc. Can you understand now why I've been hesitant telling you, wondering if you would run away and think me delusional? Falling in love with you was easy. The moment I saw you, I knew."

"I think I fell in love the moment I saw your kind, twinkling eyes in the restaurant. The twinkling is your angelness, do you think?"

"Yes, honey, I guess so."

"You are indeed blessed. Maggie told me she sees angels and they are all over the world. It is a thought I love to think about. She sees angels now like her great grandmother before her. She was with the child with special needs when she saw an angel a few years ago. Everyone knows in town that children saw angels in Mystic Bay. Do you think Maggie knows you are half angel?"

"I wonder." Alex smiles. The twinkle is still in his eyes, but the worry is gone now.

"We've finished our hot dogs so let's go out to the beach." He takes my hand and I stand but my legs feel weak as we walk out to the windy and bright seashore. He's about to give me something.

"My father proposed here two weeks after they met. I wear his wedding ring and it will be mine to wear again the day we marry." He takes the ring off and says, "Please hold this ring for me. Now -- it's time."

I can hardly speak as he gets down on one knee and takes out a ring from his pocket. "My future wife, my angel on earth, as you marry me, will you wear this ring my father gave my mother on this very beach?" It's a diamond ring in white gold. He places it on my finger, and it fits.

"It's beautiful."

Out of another pocket, Alex takes the shell shaped like a ring. My eyes have teared, my heart is filled, and I close my eyes, thanking God and His angels. He puts it on my other finger, next to the diamond ring. We look up at the sky at the same time. A rainbow has appeared to seal our love.

......

Aunt Nancy and Uncle Dick's garden is ready. August is beautiful in their bejeweled garden with summer flowers blooming and roses of different colors. In attendance are my parents, brother Julian, his wife and son, and Donnie and Laurjean. Maggie is my maid of honor and Noah is Alex's best man. We decide yellow is the theme since the sun warms our world and it's Alex's favorite color. Magic wears a collar of yellow crinoline, Ralph wears a yellow bowtie, as does Maurice, who tries to rub it off on people legs. Everyone was asked to wear something yellow, so Alex chose a white suit with a yellow tie and white and yellow striped shirt. Dad, Noah, Uncle Dick, Donnie, and Julian decided to follow suit. My mother wears a yellow lace sleeveless sheath, Maggie stuns in a yellow chiffon short dress, and Aunt Nancy looks lovely in a yellow floral dress.

And me? Well, I chose a dress I've looked at for a while in the window of a tiny boutique near the station. It came on sale the day I went in; another meant-to-be. It's a white lace, off-the-shoulder, long dress with long sleeves. It's simple, yet elegant. My hair is down and I carry yellow roses. Our favorite man of faith, Reverend Carlos Manuel, our minister from the Garden Methodist Church, performs our short ceremony. The birds in the garden sing to us as the unusual warm sea winds grace our presence. During the ceremony, Maurice perched himself in a wicker chair on the patio. He's resigned himself to wearing his bow tie, and his yellow eyes match our theme. I know the angels are near, I just can't see them. I close my eyes feeling my dad, Joe, near me. Alex whispers that he sees his parents in the garden, smiling with pride. As we say the words we've chosen, "Grow old with me, the best is yet to be," I realize, my life's journey has been filled with love and now, as we marry, I know. I've married my partner in this gift of life, my best friend.

Chapter 21

As September Leaves The Trial Begins

I've been called as the first witness. The courtroom is packed as the jury sits, six men, six women. The judge, young Honorable Ronald Fareness, walks in and we all stand. My mother sits next to me. Alex, the next witness, is on my other side.

Beau is on the other side of Alex, oddly enough. He's aware Alex and I are married and said a not so convincing "Congratulations" when we entered the courtroom. He looked over at me with a sad smile.

Evelyn Parker is charged with attempted first-degree murder.

In an amazing turn of events, Gino Carmeletti is in the room as a witness for the defense. What will he say? We are not privy to this information. What is Evelyn's defense? She sits next to her brazen and bully lawyer, Victor Vayne. She is wearing little makeup, a blue suit, and a white, high-collared lace blouse that makes her look like a school marm of yesteryear. That's not her glam style. Her hair is pulled back in an unflattering bun. The look on her face is one of sorrow, not the anger I anticipated. Nick, the heartless lover, comes in late with a woman. They sit in the back row. Tyler Parker is in our row, as well as Donnie Whitefeather. Maggie and Noah and Aunt Nancy and Uncle Dick are in the courtroom along with Breezy Bob. Sandra Garcia is a witness, and Tyler, Tory Rios, and Dr. Burns may be called.

Katerina Lopez stands and begins her opening statement. "On the night of July tenth, Evelyn Parker guided her husband, Dr. Jeremiah T. Parker, out of the casita where he was staying all alone at night. Mrs. Parker told her ailing husband that his late wife, Harriet, would be waiting by the pool. As our witnesses will prove, Evelyn Parker lead Dr. Parker by the arm and would have pushed him in the pool but Detective Beau Bolton of the San Francisco Police Department shouted her name. As she turned around, Mr. Alex Knight ran to Dr. Parker's aide and prevented him from going into the pool by catching him as he moved forward. The prosecution will prove this was a premeditated act of attempted first degree murder."

Katrina Lopez sits, and slimy Victor Vayne stands. In his gruff voice, he says, "Ladies and gentlemen of the jury, Mrs. Evelyn Parker loves her husband dearly. Thus, we will prove that Dr. Parker asked her to help him walk to the pool because he was confused and thought his late wife, Harriet, and an angel were waiting. But the so-called psychic couple were lurking outside the gate, waiting, frightening Mrs. Parker when she heard them. Mrs. Parker heard her name shouted by Detective Beau Bolton. She was startled and her husband simply lost his balance." Victor Vayne is clearly satisfied with his opening statement, dressed in a very expensive navy-blue suit, white shirt, and a tie adorned with sharks. His bald head reflects the enormous florescent light above him. Beau has stated that Victor Vayne's reputation precedes him as a high-priced defense attorney with a wealthy, cult-like following. He is known to manipulate his clients' accusers with venomous strategies. Usually, they receive somewhat lighter sentences if convicted. The judge is quite young, apparently, thirty-five, but my hope is he is as smart and savvy as Katrina Lopez has indicated to us.

I'm called as the first witness by Katrina Lopez. She's not only striking looking with Latina beauty but brilliant as well. She wears a dress Evelyn would admire, a white wool wrap with blue earrings, necklace, and blue shoes to match.

After I swear to tell the truth, I sit down.

I'm wearing black pants and a blue blouse, ironically the color of Evelyn's suit. My hair is down. Doc is safe at Tyler and Pam's home with Sandra and Eduardo as caregivers, but today someone else is caring for him. Now that Doc is in a family environment, his mind is clearer and he has made improvements walking with PT. It really is a miracle.

Katrina Lopez begins, "Mrs. Knight, Please explain to the jury exactly what transpired on June first of this year."

"That night, as on many nights, I was visited by an angel. Usually, she calms my fears or troubles of the day with her presence, but this night was different. I saw a man walking slowly toward the edge of a pool. Then I saw someone's hand on him, ready to push him in the pool, but I couldn't tell who it was. The next day, I saw a photo of Doctor Jeremiah Parker on a large screen at a fundraiser for Somerset House. I knew then that the man I saw on the screen, Dr. Jeremiah Parker, was the man in my dream. Dr. Parker said 'Angel' in my dream and although I didn't know how, I knew I had to help stop this from happening."

"Objection. You want us to believe this woman is a psychic. A premonition in a dream is not sufficiently reliable to charge Mrs. Parker with attempted murder. This is a preposterous and ridiculous farce!"

"Objection overruled," says Judge Fareness.

Katrina Lopez ignores Victor Vayne and her smooth delivery continues, "Mrs. Knight, please continue. What happened next?"

"I contacted Detective Beau Bolton of the San Francisco Police. He thought it was not something for the police to pursue. I met with Donnie Whitefeather, the former Chief of Police of Mystic Bay. He gave me attorney Alex Knight's name to speak to as Mr. Knight had helped the police with his intuition on previous occasions. I called him and we met. I explained I thought Mrs. Evelyn Parker might be planning to harm her husband. Mr. Knight believed me and investigated Evelyn Parker's background, and found there were shades of criminal behavior in her past. Together, with the help of Donnie Whitefeather, San Francisco Chief of Police Peter Warren, and Detective Beau Bolton, we formed a plan to save Dr. Parker from harm by being pushed in the pool by Evelyn Parker."

"There was an alarming experience you encountered with Evelyn Parker. Please tell us about it."

"The night of July seventh, Evelyn Parker surprised me as I was unlocking my front door. She accused me of spreading a lie to her assistant, Tory Rios, that she was neglecting her husband."

"What did you say?"

Beady-eyed, Victor Vayne stands, "Objection, hearsay! This is hearsay. There was no witness to this event."

"Overruled," says the judge.

"Go on. "

"There was a witness. My Uncle Dick, who lives with my aunt next door to me. He came out of his house after hearing Mrs. Parker yell at me and me tell her I was going to call 911. Uncle Dick saw her knock the phone out of my hand and run to her car. We saw Evelyn Parker's black Mercedes speed away."

Katrina Lopez asks, "How did you know when Dr. Parker would be led to the pool by Mrs. Parker?"

"It just came to me. My mind works that way."

"Objection! The jury deserves an explanation of this psychic ability."

Judge Fareness states, "Sustained. Please continue speaking of this ability, Mrs. Knight."

"It happens to many people who have the ability of intuition. All people have it, it's just some of us tap into that part of the brain. That's how I see it."

Victor Vane is smug, and his grimace-filled face is staring directly in my eyes. I look at him and say, "Many people have this ability, including my mother, Marie Russo Force."

"And what did she do with her psychic abilities?"

"Helpful information came to her mind in a San Francisco case when she least expected it. She concentrated on a case she dreamed of just like I did. My mother helped solve the missing child case, the April Sorenson kidnapping, twenty-eight years ago." There are gasps from the courtroom. Victor Vayne seems extremely surprised at this news.

Katrina stands. "Mrs. Knight, tell us again your dream and exactly where you were when you knew it was the night Dr. Parker would be pushed in the pool."

"I saw him being directed using his walker, a hand on his arm. I could tell someone was guiding him. I could see his face clearly as he walked. Then he said, 'Angel'

"Then, the morning after my house was broken into, I had a dream that Evelyn would walk him to the pool that night and what time it was going to happen. I told Alex Knight. He called Donnie Whitefeather and Detective Beau Bolton, and we made a plan.

"Detective Bolton was in front of the house with his men and my husband and I were waiting by the fence in the back of the house. We had walked up the path behind the house. When Doc and Evelyn Parker came out of the house, we signaled Detective Bolton on our phone. As she walked Dr. Parker to the pool, we overheard him say 'Harriet Angel.' As they neared the edge, I touched a big branch by accident and Mrs. Parker turned her attention to me. Then she stopped walking with him completely. Detective Bolton called out her name, she turned, and Alex rushed forward as the doctor began to teeter. Alex put his arms around Dr. Parker, keeping him from falling in the pool."

"Did you meet Doctor Parker, previously?"

"Yes, my mother and father told me that we met him and his wife at his son's birthday party years ago. I was three years old. Dr. Parker told them I was special and would help him some day."

"Do you think Dr. Parker has psychic abilities?"

"Yes, I do. I think he called to me in a dream the night the angel showed me the scenario."

"Objection," says Victor Vayne. "This is utter folly and fantasy. Dr. Parker is not here to speak to this nonsense."

"Overruled."

Katrina doesn't miss a beat: "Thank you, Mrs. Knight. Your witness."

"Well, well, well, Mrs. Knight. Your previous name and job, correct me if I'm wrong, is Gayle Force. You were Weather Girl on TV KHBW station, correct?"

"I am a certified meteorologist, Mr. Vayne. I'm now on leave for this trial, and I have taken my husband's last name."

"Ah, and you and your husband are psychics, correct?" He turns to the jury with a smirk on his face.

"Yes."

"You think you have the power to foresee the future, like you have a crystal ball, I assume?"

"Objection," says Katrina Lopez. "Mr. Vayne is badgering the witness."

"Sustained," says Judge Fareness.

"You saw this in your dream, got police and your future psychic husband to believe you, and one night, as Mrs. Parker took her husband out for fresh air by the pool, there you are with your made-up dream story?"

"Objection, badgering again, your Honor."

The judge calls the two attorneys to the bench. Mr. Vayne seems upset. I can hear the judge in low tones chastising him. Mr. Vayne turns to me angrily: "No more questions."

I step down as gracefully as possible but feel my legs shaking. I do not look at Evelyn or Victor Vayne. I look directly at my mother, then father, then dear Alex. Katrina Lopez calls her next witness, Alex Knight. As he stands up, I catch his eye and I smile. I hold my composure as much as possible. Alex is sworn in.

"Mr. Knight, tell us exactly how you came to know Mrs. Knight, formerly, Ms. Force, in the days leading up to this incident." As Alex explains, corroborating everything I have just said, he explains that he's worked on several cases with the San Francisco Police Department. He's very convincing. When asked when he understood himself to be psychic, he answers, "I refer to myself as intuitive. My late father was Tobias Knight of the San Francisco Police Department. He actually worked with my mother-in-law, Marie Russo Force, on the April Sorenson case in 1995. I met Marie when I started dating my wife."

"Did you believe Gayle's story and abilities when you first met?"

"Yes, she is extremely intuitive, and her intuition is escalating.

"Tell us about your investigation into Evelyn Parker's past."

Alex relays all he knows: her engagement to Nick Carmeletti, her marriage and the money stolen from her former father-in-law, and the diamond incident at Everett and Dixie Pomeroy's home. "Her second husband would not talk to me."

"Your witness, Mr. Vayne."

The overbearing lawyer struts over to Alex and turns around to the jury. "Mr. Knight, you're an intuitive man, so you say. Well now, weren't you thinking when you met your future wife that you'd like to date this pretty morning weather TV personality?"

"Objection your Honor."

"Sustained."

"I'll rephrase it. Had you seen your wife on TV before you met in person?"

"Yes, I had."

"And you teamed up because you believed her? Wow, a husband-and-wife psychic detective team, how interesting. No further questions. You may step down, Mr. Knight."

Katrina says, "I call Mrs. Sandra Garcia to the stand."

Dear Sandra Garcia, dressed in a maroon dress and heels, comes forward. Her graying black shiny hair is swept up perfectly in a long ponytail. Her hoop earrings were a present, she told me, from Tyler and Pam. She takes the oath. "Mrs. Garcia, please explain your duties at the Parker household."

"I was part of a cleaning crew for Dr. and Mrs. Parker for five years but when Dr. Parker got sick, she asked me to take care of him. Me and my husband were glad to help the good doctor."

"And in the last six weeks, what has transpired? "

"Mrs. Parker didn't feed him too good, just those prepared home meals that come to the door every day. So I sneak in ham sandwiches and handmade bean burritos every day too. She didn't pay my husband enough to have him help Dr. Parker take a shower, but Eduardo came anyway because we love Doctor. I couldn't lift him myself. I didn't give him all the pills she wanted me to give him. I put them in my purse in a plastic bag every day. I only give him the pills from Dr. Burns. Dr. Burns come to check him out every week and say he was gaining weight because I'm good at his care."

"What else did Dr. Burns say?"

"He tell me Eduardo and I do good for him. I heard him tell Mrs. Parker that Doctor should go, would do better to go to rehab, but she didn't want to. She didn't have nobody to help after six at night and so I tucked Doctor in, and I don't know if she check on him all night."

"Objection," says Victor Vayne.

"Overruled. Keep going Mrs. Garcia."

"She ask me every day if I give Doctor all his pills. I lie and say yes because I didn't want to give him those extra pills."

Katrina looks at the jury. "Note the evidence being handed to the judge. It is the purse with the plastic bag of sixty-two pills. Two for every day the doctor was living in the casita. The lab notes they are Opioids, used for pain, and are addicting."

"Objection, Your Honor. How do we know Mrs. Garcia didn't plant them there?"

Sandra Garcia's husband stands up and shouts in Spanish, "Mentiroso! Ella no tiene corazon!"

"What is he saying?" the judge asks Katrina.

"He is saying, 'Liar. The woman has no heart!'"

The courtroom fills with noise and chatter.

"Order in the court!" Judge Fareness is furious. Sandra starts crying, looking at the judge. "I tell the truth, Judge. I kept them from Doctor, because my mind says they are bad for him."

The judge hands Sandra the tissue box.

Katrina continues, "Mrs. Garcia, please tell us about your call to Gayle Force Knight."

"She so pretty. We watch her every morning on TV, Doctor and me. He call her his Angel. So, I call her up at her TV work. She said to call her anytime and then she tell me next time we talk she would help Doctor leave the house and go to Tyler." Katrina says, "Your witness."

Victor seems unsettled by this news. "Did Mrs. Parker tell you to give Dr. Parker those extra pills?"

"No, she just said they were extra."

"No further questions."

Sandra Garcia steps down and doesn't look at Evelyn Parker, but most of the jury does. They are staring at the woman with no heart. But is Eduardo correct about Evelyn? I am getting the feeling something is very wrong with this trial.

We break for lunch and Evelyn is taken away. My family go to a local diner we know and eat, hungry for something to fill our upset stomachs. Grilled cheese, hamburgers, and fries are the answer. We don't talk about the trial, of course. We are all on edge. But I can't eat. I keep having misgivings about Evelyn. What am I thinking? She didn't mean to harm him?

When we return, Katrina Lopez says in a relaxed tone, "I call Detective Beau Bolton." For some reason, Beau looks at me as he walks up. His story matches Alex's and mine. "I should have listened to Gayle when she first told me. I know now I was wrong. I yelled her name and Evelyn Parker stopped short from pushing her husband in the pool. He teetered and Alex saved him from falling in."

Victor Vayne seems nervous and doesn't cross-examine.

Tyler Parker is called. He relates how Evelyn kept him from his father and that his father was angry when Tyler didn't react well to his marrying Evelyn. When his father became ill and she took over, Tyler left Somerset House. He kept in touch with Dr. Burns, who said everything was going fine but he thought it would be best for Dr. Parker to go to rehab. Tyler had still not spoken to his father because he didn't want to see Evelyn.

Victor was, of course, rude to Tyler. "Weren't you so upset about his marrying Evelyn that you stopped speaking to your father and made an uncomfortable situation at the company? You were always rude to Evelyn. Then when Mrs. Parker took over, you left."

"Yes. He seemed to love her more than he loved me."

"No further questions."

We see Tory Rios take the stand, explaining how she overheard Evelyn making love talk with Nick Carmeletti. She explains how she spoke to me on the phone that night, as she knew Evelyn would come find me at my home. "I feel so bad I told her Gayle was asking if she was neglecting her husband."

Victor Vayne cross-examines, "Why would you do that? If you are a good assistant, private phone calls to your boss are just that, private."

"I worried about Doc," she says in tears.

The next witness is hostile Nick Carmeletti. He is wearing a shiny black suit, black shirt, white tie, and black, pointed, lizard shoes. He looks like he'd fit right into the movie *The Godfather*. After he swears to tell the truth, Katrina says in a strong voice, "Mr. Carmeletti, are you lovers with Mrs. Parker?"

"Certainly not,'\" he lies. "She's been following me around and begging me to be her lover for thirty years."

"Then if this is true, then why did Miss Tory Rios hear a phone call where Mrs. Parker said, and I quote, "Nick, I love you too"?

"The girl must not have heard correctly," he says smugly.

This is the first time we see Evelyn's face change. She goes from frightened to white and faints in the chair. We have a short break. So far, it doesn't look good for Evelyn.

But who would believe that the final surprise witness is none other than my intruder, Guiseppi Grimaldi.

He looks neat in a suit and his hair is recently cut. He's another one who looks at me as he approaches to take the oath.

Katrina plays him like a fiddle, "Mr. Grimaldi. You broke into Gayle Force Knight's home. Why?"

"She's been in the restaurant. I wanted to see her up close, sleeping. She's nice, and such a beauty. She was the only customer to give me a big tip even though I'm usually rude to customers. She had a brown wig on the night she came in, but days later I overheard Evelyn lady on trial and Nick talk about her, who she was, how she was wearing a wig. I see her on TV. I just wanted to see her, and check that she was okay."

"And, you have something else to tell us."

'Yeah. I dropped off a bunch of drugs about a month ago to that lady, Evelyn's, house on Sea Grape Circle in Hillsboro." He points to Evelyn. "I was sent by my boss, Nick there." He points to Nick. Obviously, Guiseppi is getting a lighter sentence for this.

Nick stands and screams, "This man is a liar! I fired him weeks ago!" The pretty, exotic young woman next to him stands also. She's dressed like a lady of the evening, as my grandmother used to say.

Gino Carmeletti stands and yells, "Nick, you are the liar! Tell them Evie! Tell them who the real bad guy is. Nick Carmeletti! He's got you in trouble for years!"

The judge pounds his gavel. "Order, order in the court." As the loud talking of the crowd dies down, Katrina Lopez looks at the jury. "The prosecution rests."

Chapter 22

Dreams Come One More Time

My dream is filled with sorrow. My angel is pointing to a scene from the past months. Evelyn is in the casita, looking at her husband, a sleeping Doc. The moon shines in the window. She's been crying. She whispers, "You saved me, Jeremiah. I don't want anything to happen to you. I don't want to do what Nick says." She gets in his bed with him and places her hand on his. I awaken and shoot up in bed. Alex wakes up, "What's wrong, honey?"

"Oh my, I've been wrong, we've all been wrong!!"

We arrange a meeting with the Alex and me, the judge, Katrina, and Victor. I tell them my dream and they all listen and believe me. Judge Fareness calls for a recess. We know now that Evelyn did not ever want to hurt Jeremiah. After she'd get home at night, she would slip into the casita and stay with him most nights, except when Nick would come over urging her to do Jeremiah harm. There is more, and we have a plan brewing for how to proceed.

It's two p.m. Victor calls his first witness, Evelyn. Evelyn comes up to the witness stand, tears in her eyes, her lips turned down in sorrow. Victor is soft in his delivery. "Mrs. Parker, please tell us your version of your husband's care and the night in question."

"I took care of him, hiring Sandra, and she and Eduardo did a good job. I knew she was bringing food, which was fine; I knew she wouldn't give him those pills Nick wanted me to give him. I knew she would throw them out or flush them in the toilet. Nick was mad and told me I should make Sandra give Jeremiah those pills so he would sleep most of the day. But I didn't.

"Oh God, please forgive me. I was always doing what Nick wanted me to. He told me to steal the diamond jewels he gave Dixie Pomeroy when they were engaged. Years ago, he had me marry my first husband and get him a key to the office of Baxter Mellon, my father-in-law. He always promised we'd be together, but it never happened. He told me he loved me, and once Jeremiah was gone and I inherited the money, he would finally marry me in Chicago at the Kedzie Mansion. He said he gambled all his money away like his father did and he needed my money. I was always giving him money."

Her tears are coming in a stream of sadness. Victor goes on, "Did you intend to kill your husband, Dr. Jeremiah Parker?"

"No. He was calling angels and Harriet and wanted to walk out to the pool that night. It was like he knew someone was out there. Nick told me to take him to the pool and push him in some night, but I didn't want to. He kept calling me and demanding it. That night, Jeremiah insisted and got up himself, almost falling. I decided I would walk with him because he wanted to see an angel and Harriet. I would have stopped him from falling. I could never harm him. I hoped the angels would really come. I was relieved when I heard Gayle and her husband by the bushes but scared when Detective Bolton shouted my name. I would never kill anybody. They not only saved Jeremiah, they saved me too." Then in a weakened voice, "Please, God knows I am telling the truth."

"Did Nick Carmeletti, your former fiancé, ask you to lead Jeremiah to your pool and push him in?"

"Yes," She weeps.

We look in the back of the courtroom. Nick is trying to leave, leaving his girlfriend sitting there, but is stopped by the guards.

"Thank you," says Katrina. "Your witness."

"No questions."

"I call Gino Carmeletti to the stand."

Gino walks up, looking at Evelyn, takes his oath, and sits down.

"Tell us all you know about Evelyn Parker and Nick Carmeletti, your twin brother."

"I don't consider him my brother anymore. He has ruined Evelyn's life. He has kept her like a puppet on a string for many years. He rejected her then coerced her into marrying Baxter Mellon, Jr., when she was only eighteen, and he made her help him steal Baxter's father's money. She stole jewelry from Dixie, his former fiancé. He had gambling debts he made her pay, all the while telling her they'd be together someday. She would never harm Jeremiah. He was kind to her and tried to help her when she got in trouble. She hired Sandra, a caring woman. She was with him every night after she'd come home, about eight. But she was infatuated with the lascivious narcissist, and I was in love with her for years. Evelyn," he looks at her. "You chose the wrong brother."

Evelyn weeps.

"No further questions," says Katrina Lopez, who like all of us is on edge and stunned.

A recess is called.

Alex and I are in the Judge Ron Fareness' chambers with Katrina Lopez, Victor Vayne, Tyler Parker, and Detective Beau Bolton. Evelyn has been released and comes in, looking thin and frightened, with Gino Carmeletti. The case will be dismissed. All parties are in agreement. Evelyn cried in Gino's arms.

Later, as we sit outside, the Honorable Judge Ron Fareness addresses the closed courtroom, with only the jury present. We learned later that he told them, "The charges against Mrs. Parker are dropped. Thank you for your time." The reporters swarm the stairs and the front doors of the courthouse. Victor Vayne and Katrina Lopez walk out together as Evelyn leaves through the back with Gino Carmeletti.

Katrina announces to the reporters: "The Honorable Ron Fareness has ruled. All charges are dropped. Mrs. Parker is free."

With only a very few people knowing, Guiseppi Grimaldi, per his agreement to turn state's evidence against Nick, is a government witness. He will testify against Nick with all he knows about his drug business. He knows he is a walking dead man unless the government can protect him through the Witness Protection program. We know there will be justice for Dr. Jeremiah Parker because now Nick will be indicted on many counts.

Chapter 23
Summer And Fall Turn To Winter

Months have gone by since the trial ended. Doc is back in his own home, doing well with his live-in caregivers, Sandra and Eduardo. His relationship with Tyler is back to the wonderful father and son union. Evelyn is in therapy and she and Doc amicably divorced. Doc paid all her attorney fees because he didn't blame her. Apparently, Evelyn continues to become a softer person and Gino Carmeletti is always by her side. It's a blessing that I had the nagging feeling and dream that Evelyn didn't plan to harm her husband. But Doc knew it wasn't her planning, he knew Nick was scheming. His stroke had prevented him from expressing his concern, so he contacted me in my dream by way of an angel.

Nick? He's facing prison on drug dealing, tax evasion, and most importantly, attempted murder.

My new position at KHWB is another dream job. Weather on the weekend mornings with Magic, The Weather Dog, and producing and reporting weekly special segments called, "Good News Around the Bay." So, weekdays I get to have coffee with my husband before he goes to work. Happily, I'm known as Gayle Knight, now, and it feels just right.

But tonight, it's Christmas, and Maggie and Noah have asked us to meet them at eleven thirty on this very chilly Mystic Bay night at Dog Beach. It's late for us after a full Christmas dinner with our family, but we are here, bundled up with Magic and Ralph, both wearing their plaid winter jackets as well.

We're wondering what they want to show us on this star-filled night. We figure it's the bright, full Christmas moon, stars, or a meteor shower. Either way, it's a beautiful time to watch the universe from the sandy beach, with the waves' soothing sounds filling our souls. Maggie and Noah walk toward us in the moonlight, as clad for the cold weather as we are. Their smiles welcome us, their friendship everlasting.

Noah says, "This is a night you will never forget, Alex and Gayle. Maggie has been told it is time."

Alex says, "What do you mean? Time for what?" We look at each other, wondering what's up.

Maggie says to Alex, "Last night, I had a Christmas Eve vision of your mother, Rachel. She is such a beautiful angel, with wings made of starlight. She told me you are a half angel, Alex."

Overwhelmed, Alex says, "Yes, I am. You saw her?"

"Yes, and she told me you need to know the truth about Mystic Bay, but it is a secret meant to be kept. There are many angels living as humans in town. Since you are married to Gayle, you both are witness tonight to the miracle that happens in Mystic Bay"

I am speechless but Alex asks, "It's incredible! Are they people we know?"

"Yes, you know them all. But, now it's time," says Maggie taking my hand. "Don't be afraid, dear Gayle. You have seen angels in your dreams, and Alex, you see the spirit of your father and angel mother. Look to the south now, for they will come. This is the exact spot we saw them for the first time three years ago ourselves."

We look to the south not seeing anything at first but hearing a sound like the wings of sea birds in flight. We hear the sound then see a swirling cloud of glittering silver, moving toward us, twenty feet above us. They are not birds, but angels! Each angels' magnificent wings are so different from each other. In blinding beauty, they fly toward us.

It's an amazing sight to see as our dear friend, Donnie, is leading the flight of angels. His golden wings spread six feet tip-to-tip. We both kneel to the ground with our dogs at our sides in wonderment. There are others.

Our vet, Josh, comes towards us with blue iridescent wings. We feel the light wind emanating from his wings as he glides. He waves and others follow. We recognize all eight angels from town. We are surprised to see Donnie and Josh.

Five males and three females rise in synchronicity, their faces gleaming in the night. They are all dressed in white, their eyes have a star shine like no other. They fly down the beach as quickly as they came, turning north. Their swirling cloud of silver and glitter is gone in a moment in time.

Maggie says, "They fly to San Francisco to help those in need tonight. It's their mission on Saturday nights, and on Christmas Eve and Christmas night, of course."

I find I'm crying, having seen a miracle. "We have been given a gift, Maggie and Noah. We've seen the flight of angels, and to think they are living as humans in our seaside town!"

Alex says, "Did you see Magic and Ralph? They looked up, they saw the angels, too."

Maggie says, "Animals have always seen angels."

We are blessed knowing and living near angels. It was my angel who placed Magic at my door that night. She knew I needed another furry companion to love. Alex was sent to me by his angel mother and his dear father. We stay awhile, taking in what we have witnessed. We know we are fortunate to live in Mystic Bay, the Town of Angels, where there is a secret only a very few can know. Angels live as humans here. They do good works, guiding their flocks of humans, loving their earthly families, and enjoying their lives, both celestial and earthbound.

We say goodnight and hug our dear friends with thankful words. Alex and I walk home hand-in-hand. Alex holds Magic in his other arm, and I have Ralph on a leash by my side. We are ready for the warmth of our home. There's a cat named Maurice waiting for us. A fire is in the fireplace, and oh, what a secret we have now that needs keeping. All over the world tonight, angels live as humans helping those in need. Our world is awash with angels. Have you ever seen one? Now, I have, and I can say, BELIEVE in angels. They're all around us.

Acknowledgments

It is with great appreciation I express my gratitude to the following people who support my writing with their knowledge, guidance, and creativity. Thank you to Don McCauley, my publicist, who always believes in my writing and promotes me and gets the word out to the world. Don formats my books and helps fix any problems along the way. He has created the perfect website for me.

I would like to thank Barbara Youngs, my amazing editor. With expertise, wit and encouraging kindness, she helped me create a wonderful manuscript. I thank those who always inspire me as characters in my books. Maggie is patterned after my own dear angel-like friend Maggie, who inspires me with her kind being. Laurjean was created in honor of my dear friend Laura – our bond and friendship are everlasting. In Summer of Angels, Aunt Nancy and Uncle Dick and their dog, Prince, are indeed patterned after Nancy and Dick, the dearest of friends for many years and their wonderful rescue dog, Prince.

Gayle in my stories is patterned after dear friend, Sharyn G. (Gayle) Jordan, author and storyteller extraordinaire.

Magic, the dog, was inspired by meeting Amy Ahrensdorf, author of It Had to Be Magic, and meeting her wonderful dog, Magic, the star of her book. My sister Karen reads all my manuscripts, and her input is invaluable. At her suggestion, I turned this novel into a Mystic Bay Mystery. The angel Susan in my book is named after my dear friend Susan Claire Anderson, who is a children's book author and who illustrated my children's book, When The Angel Sent Butterflies.

I appreciate my children Mike and Elizabeth for their ongoing support and love for me and my work. To my grandchildren, Jones and Kate, characters in my children's book, I send love always. Last but not least I thank my husband, Dave. His suggestions are always welcome. He chose Nick's mafia-like outfits and helped in many ways with ideas for dialog in the trial as we both grew up watching Perry Mason.

Thank you to my readers, past and present for the reviews and love for the characters and town of Mystic Bay.